# INTIMATIONS OF DEATH

Felix Timmermans was born in Lier, Belgium in 1886, the thirteenth of fourteen children in the family of a lace merchant. Largely self-taught, he left school at 15 and began to read widely while also pursuing art lessons. Although best known today for his writing, Timmermans was also an accomplished painter and graphic artist and often provided illustrations to his own books.

Timmermans' novels of Flemish rural life, usually written in a light-hearted or humorous vein, proved tremendously popular not only with Dutch readers but also internationally, being translated into twenty-seven languages. His first major success was *Pallieter* (1916), an 'ode to life' written after a moral and physical crisis and warmly received by the public in the wake of the misery of World War I. The story of Pallieter, a miller who enjoys the simple, natural life to the full, the novel's mixture of abundant humour and keen observation of rural life won many admirers, including Stefan Zweig, Rainer Maria Rilke, and Hermann Hesse, and sold more than a million copies internationally.

Timmermans' other well-known works included romanticized biographies of Pieter Bruegel and St Francis of Assisi, and his novel *A Peasant's Psalm* (1935), which was filmed in 1989. He died in 1947.

Paul Vincent studied at Cambridge and in Amsterdam. Until 1989 he was a professor in the Dutch department of University College London. Since then he has worked as a freelance translator. His translations include works by Louis Couperus, Harry Mulisch, Arnon Grunberg, Louis Paul Boon and many others. He has received a number of awards for his translation work, including the David Reid Poetry Translation Prize and the Vondel Prize.

Felix Timmermans

# INTIMATIONS OF DEATH

*Translated from the Dutch by*
PAUL VINCENT

VALANCOURT BOOKS

*Intimations of Death* by Felix Timmermans
Originally published in Dutch as *Schemeringen van den Dood* in 1910
First Valancourt Books edition 2019



'The White Vase' originally appeared in *The Dedalus Book of Flemish Fantasy* in 2011 and is reprinted by kind permission of Dedalus Books.

Published by Valancourt Books, Richmond, Virginia
http://www.valancourtbooks.com



ISBN 978-1-948405-40-9 (*trade paperback*)

Also available as an electronic book.

This book was published with the generous support of Flanders Literature (flandersliterature.be).

FLANDERS LITERATURE

All Valancourt Books publications are printed on acid free paper that meets all ANSI standards for archival quality paper.

Set in Dante MT

# CONTENTS

# INTRODUCTION

Felix Timmermans was born in the Belgian city of Lier in 1886 and died there in 1947. Lier stands at a confluence of rivers, and the ancient centre is still surrounded by water. The countryside flows away in all directions and was always to be present in Timmermans' work. His first books started to appear in the years before the outbreak of World War I. The majority of them would be poetry and novels; however, his third book was a collection of stories, *Intimations of Death* (*Schemeringen van den dood*), first published in 1910. Although these five stories lack the unity of a single extended work, they do nevertheless possess cohesion. This is due not only to their common themes, but also through their setting. A note at the end of the book states 'These stories were written in Lier, 1909'. Whether or not the stories in *Intimations of Death* were the product of some sort of extended trance or fever dream, they certainly read as if they could have been.

Reading Timmermans, we never seem to stray far from the Flemish landscape in which he was born, lived, and died. As could be expected from a group of stories sharing a common setting, there is much recurring imagery: fields, rivers, lakes, avenues of trees, isolated houses, farms. Their old and decaying buildings are outside the city walls, and set out in the open, off small roads and lanes. It always seems to be autumn.

The weather is always stormy. Water is everywhere; everything seems damp; it is often raining or snowing.

In these stories he portrays and defines his native region with the skill of an author who saw and observed with the eye of an artist. And so it is perhaps not surprising that as well as being a prolific writer, Timmermans also drew and painted. In the stories, words substitute for, and take on, a painting's lines and masses of colour and gloom; and if the illustrations that accompany the stories comprising *Intimations of Death* are also by their author, as is possible, nothing could be more appropriate. In their stark and brutal simplicity they have a Gothic intensity, matching that of the stories, recalling those series of woodcuts depicting the Dance of Death: so popular, so troubling – and so true. (At this point, rightly, we must salute the art of the translator, too.)

Timmermans is fond of putting the reader at something of a distance from the events recounted, as if they were seen by the reader being made to gaze through the wrong end of a telescope. Yet he never sacrifices immediacy. Everything seems to be happening now, close by, with immediate and startling effect. For example, at the very outset of 'The Mourner' the writer of the opening sentence immediately hands over to his friend, whose account the story becomes. The new narrator's mother is dying in the old stone-built family home, every room of which is full of strange noises. The house stands next to an avenue of trees which serves no apparent purpose in the wide, flat landscape. It is also surrounded by a moat full of water. The narrator has spent his life bound to this house, as if tied to it through the souls of the dead siblings he has seen die and taken away from it to be buried. Death soon intrudes again and surrounds, too, and a kind of bargain is struck. The presence of Death is normal, a companion. Timmermans employs symbols that make clear its reach and effects. A similar device frames the narrative of 'The Cellar', which is the longest story here. The apparent narrator finds a sealed and much-addressed letter, which he cannot resist opening. In short order he presents its text to the reader. The writer of the letter describes his romance with Mina – a heightened, obsessive, relationship worthy of Edgar Allan Poe. Their marriage is to be one of souls only. And not only that, but within the walls of another Usheresque house: 'We could not imagine our future without that house. It seemed as fatally predestined for us as life and death.' But in an ideal marriage of souls it turns out that the physical is not to be denied, after all.

In these stories we are taken in from the start and carried off by Timmermans' intense, tortured narratives. He went on to write many novels that celebrated life in the Flemish countryside; but he started off, here, by celebrating Death. And Timmermans celebrates it (him?) in such a way as few others ever did, including Poe. The 'intimations' of Death often seem to be misnomers. Those intimations are frequently the opposite. In 'The Seventh Grave' it seems that the trappings of the dead, and so Death, are there for the narrator's pleasure. He befriends a gravedigger, whose story this also becomes: 'I feel for each gravedigger something between admiration and fear, because does he not live on Death? He is a higher being than all of us, a man with a supernatural vocation, an intermediary between God and Death.' The narrator realises that Death is everywhere. But he sees that the gravedigger's office assures him against Death: he is in effect a collaborator, who alone of everyone else is able to enter Death's territory – and leave it again. In 'The Unknown' a young couple 'crushed by life' have fallen in love with Death and plan to die together. Being dead would be the only way to ensure they could be together and enjoy their love. But their plans do not unfold as they had wished, at least to begin with. Symbols abound in 'The White Vase'. The narrator is staying at a gloomy Gothic Trappist monastery. He wishes to leave, but does not. The sense of doom grows. Is it the approach of Death? And will he be able to evade Death?

All the great tropes of horror are displayed in *Intimations of Death*: all the stuff of Gothic literature as it could only be conceived and loved in the age of candles and gaslight giving way to the hard electric illumination of the *fin de siècle* and *Belle Époque*. But the buildings are much older relics – and not the only relics. Whoever designed them surely wished claustrophobia, at least, on those who have to inhabit them and visit them. Windows are barred, doors are locked – and the cellars are extensive. The rich – and richly bloody – religious heritage of the Low Countries is everywhere evident. Churches and churchyards form a constant part of the scene. Convents and monasteries abound.

Timmermans' narratives achieve a sense of distance and dislocation not only through their settings, with the author's impressionistic descriptions of landscape and its oddly-placed buildings and people caught (and trapped) among the rivers and netted by the roads. The storytelling is equally non-straightforward, involving the nesting of oral narratives and the use of letters. We are told who is writing or talking to us – and it isn't always who the story is actually about. Who knows what else might have become unreliable in the retellings over the passage of years?

The characters that tread warily through these stories are in the grip of forces larger than themselves as individuals. They are racked by illness and pain. Their lives and loves are doomed. They pray – and are prey. They find out by experience something that we already knew (don't we?) beyond doubt: that Death is always with us – and so a part of life, and inescapable. Towards the end of 'The Unknown' the narrator muses on his lot: 'He thought of all the vicissitudes of the past, of how everything in life was set against him. He felt like God's stepchild. Oh, it could all have gone so differently.' After reading these stories of God's stepchildren, who can say with absolute certainty that we are not their brothers and sisters?

JOHN HOWARD

JOHN HOWARD was born in London. His books include *Visit of a Ghost*, *The Silver Voices*, *Written by Daylight*, *Cities and Thrones and Powers*, and *Buried Shadows*. He has published essays on various aspects of the science fiction and horror fields, and especially on the work of classic authors such as Fritz Leiber, Arthur Machen, August Derleth, M.R. James, and writers of the pulp era. Many of these have been collected in *Touchstones: Essays on the Fantastic*.

# THE MOURNER

MY FRIEND tells the story:

'I myself am frightened now my mouth is about to tell you this.

My mother lay dying. Despair inundated me like a great mass of water flooding a broken dyke; not so much because my mother was about to enter eternity, but because she was to die in this house; this house that at night was filled with strange noises from the cellar to the attic. Oh! let me first say something about this house, so that you will know better the dreadful way that what I am going to tell you happened.

Our house stood all by itself on the bare, wide heath, alongside a tall avenue of beeches lost in dusk in the distance, which, like a dark Gothic gallery, cut across the sad wasteland at right angles.

Oh! the monotonous days and fearful years I spent there. Never did the peaceful sound of a wagon come clattering down the earth road that went on for hours, never did anyone pass our house. The avenue, without a single residence but ours along it, began a quarter of an hour outside the town walls, passed our house, and ended an hour and a half further on, in a plain as far as the eye could see, which revealed nothing but a blue horizon.

The avenue served no purpose. It lay there like something superfluous in the world. It was like a being that lived, advanced towards a goal, but had felt how useless or unattainable it was and had stopped. So, our house was lost in the infinity of earth and sky. But what had a particularly frightening effect on my mind in this thickly overarched lane was that right opposite our house there rose a white wall, above which an army of black poplars raised their black crowns, which in their thick green foliage hid a deserted convent. The rooms and the church were empty, but owls and ravens, rats and bats let their swift shadows glide across the white walls.

On the other side, giving onto the plain, a large green gate kept the only entrance permanently closed. Once I visited the convent with my elder brother. We had climbed over the wall with a ladder, but there was nothing to see but long white corridors and wide, high rooms in which our muted voices made a hollow echo. We were so terrified – we did not even know by what – that we never returned. I kept thinking that someone lived behind those walls; for sometimes such strange sounds issued from there, like groaning and the stepping of heavy feet. At night the crows and owls could sometimes make such a din that I hid under the sheets from fear . . .

The silence that hung around us was appalling and like a lead weight on the heart. Our house, built centuries ago in Kempen stone, which has the colour of congealed blood, was outlined in black against the bare horizon, along which the evening twilight died out. Oh! it stood there so mysteriously, our house, in the endless space and the silence, like a dark hovel erected to contain the dark mystery of life . . . A deep black moat, covered in green scum, enclosed the thick damp walls.

One misty morning a tramp had stumbled into it and drowned. A four-stepped bridge with an iron railing climbed to the white-painted door, in which a round barred spyhole looked into the white hall. On either side of the entrance was a deeply recessed arched window with iron bars over it, and the three wide, square windows of the only floor, where our bedrooms were. On the valerian-covered, blue-tiled roof on the right a wooden tower, without a clock, raised its peaked slate roof. There used to be one on the left too, but lightning had struck it down.

Why we stayed living there in solitude, in that dark beech avenue, opposite the white wall of an abandoned convent, I cannot tell you. The only reason was, I think, that father, grandfather and his father before him had been born there and had always lived there; that it was in our blood to live there. But those who had lived there had never been aware of the mysterious air weighing on the soul, which pressed down in the house and across the plain; but my heart was like a gate open to the unknown, and I always had the clear consciousness of another life around me.

I saw it and felt it from the white chilly walls, from the black earth, the grey sky and the gloomy avenue. I felt the soul of things like a wind around me. And this feeling, that sense of not being alone, made me afraid and life sad. I never breathed a word of this to anyone, for fear of awakening this debilitating feeling in my parents. I grew older and as I grew this feeling grew along with me. My life in that solitude passed slowly and fearfully. My mother had inherited quite a large fortune from a distant aunt, so that I did not have to work. Hence, I was always extremely bored.

My only pleasure was to see nature in action, season after season following each other, to see how summer let a feeble light into the rooms through the dark foliage of the trees, and how in winter the moonlight, stiff as static lightning, filled the halls with green. I could listen to the rain like I now listen to Wagner's music and I was as happy as a child to be able to walk in the pressure of the wild wind on the plain. Chopping wood, planting flowers, drying herbs were sometimes my activities, and in the evenings I read wonderful stories in very old books, which stimulated my mind and imagination. For whole hours I could make monotonous songs float from bagpipes over the plain. Now I am amazed that I did not flee the house! I helped carry three dead souls – a brother and two sisters – out of that dwelling and helped bury them in the distant cemetery. My dear parents were now all that was left to me, and with the three of us, my fear of life climbed higher and higher. But they, good people, were happy and had peace in their hearts. Their eyes shone with calm and their mouths were full of silent words about ordinary things or murmured prayers of thanks. No, they didn't feel it, the mysteriousness that weighed on them, nor the face of the unknown that was watching our hands.

Now my mother had become ill. It was an illness which worsened with desperate gradualness and which the strongest herbs, recommended by my old books, could not suppress. I saw how nature too lost its sunniness. The greenery was luxuriant, but dark and dry over the land. No more summer smell wafted about and the songbirds had gone overseas, so that the trees of the avenue stood there as if without souls. An intensely bright sunlight shone, which was not warm and cast sharp shadows. Nature seemed to stand still, outside life and time. But in that rest lay the restlessness of Death. So it remained for a considerable time, full of mystery, until the day when what I want to tell you about happened, the blue sky closed and darkness, full of ominous power, weighed on the mysterious world. That power unleashed itself in a ghastly succession of thunder and lightning which lit up everywhere the supplicant flame on the holy candles.

That was the sign of the summer's death! Afterwards I saw the leaves immediately become redder and fall like dead birds on the ground.

It was Fate, which with as much certainty as ease gnawed away the heart of awesome nature as that of an ant . . . And I felt as if those dark forces of the storm, like living beings, heralded in mad triumph that Death was coming for my mother. And then I began to pray for her preservation. Yet here I felt from on high the impassive power of something that is stronger than what derives from men. My praying was writing in the sand.

That morning my mother's condition had suddenly become very bad. She lay unconscious, without strength, and her breath rattled in short, laboured gasps and came out of her throat squeaking like a muffled cry for help from distant cellars. I had immediately gone for the doctor. He thought she was in a very bad state and ordered the priest to be fetched at once, but since this storm had let loose, I was forced to wait until it was over. So we would wait. And in the front room the three of us sat around the white-curtained bed, in which mother lay dying. Her head was severe as a marble church; she was white-faced with black eyes, set deep below her forehead, and had black hair, with a blue sheen like a Namur earthenware jug. She lay very still and her thin, yellow hands, on which there was a tangle of blue sinews, lay limply against her body. The last spark of her life was flickering out, and full of powerless despair we saw the most lasting and sweetest thing in our lives being snuffed out by Death, whose breath had long been wandering through our house. We were silent. The silence weighed like a black pall of smoke in the room and the mad twilight trembled like a useless thing along the high walls which were covered with a brown, symmetrical flowered wallpaper ... Mother let her head fall to the side and viewed us with such a severe, dark look, that we turned away, full of reverent fear. Did she see our souls? ... In her eyes there was already the mysterious clarity of the other world.

We did not dare look at her who was so dear to us! ... Father, the doctor and I surveyed each other with closed mouths, afraid of Death that was inside and outside. The storm raged terribly as if the whole world was about to burst open and perish in flames. The bright-green lightning blazed, putting the simple objects in a sharp light, danced on the walls, and cast a green glow onto mother's snow-white face. Then the thunder crashed and exploded with a deafening noise above our heads and tumbled drowsily with heavy jolts to the end of the world. Then the restless silence reigned again, in which only mother's laborious, wheezing breath rose and fell. It went on like that for a long, slow time and it kept renewing itself with more ferocious strength.

It was ghostly when the lightning flickered over the white convent wall, which then crept away again into the twilight, as dark as the ice in a pond. It was not raining and that made our fear even sharper. Had not one tower been toppled from the roof by such a storm? . . . The doctor drew his thick eyebrows over his eyes and peered motionlessly, suspiciously to the side, as if he kept thinking that a lightning strike was going to cause the house to collapse on his head. Father kept his eyes wide open, filled with dread, looking at the foot of the bed as if he saw Death sitting there. He kept his hands together because they were trembling so with fear. What still amazes me is that during this great moment no one made the sign of the cross . . . So we sat there in the thick twilight and did not dare to look at mother. Then I realised for the first time that people remain like children when surrounded by the unknown . . . Suddenly mother gave a short gasp. We looked up.

Her eyes were pulled shut as if with threads. We leapt up, aware that the great moment had come. Father fell on mother's breast and sobbed with pent-up words: "She's dead, good God, she's dead!" The doctor grabbed her wrist and looked with forced calm at the white ceiling. Yet to me it was as if nothing was happening. It was as if I was at a great distance and were seeing all this in a dream. I was ashamed of myself, that no great pain welled up in me and my mind did not lose its balance. I also wanted to do something, with which I could show externally a great sorrow in me. But I did not know what. Suddenly, in a flash of lightning, I saw the consecrated candle rise up trembling, like a holy thought. That gave me something to do. I lit it, and immediately there floated through the room a dusty reddish, feeble light, which spread a dull glowing hue over the glistening objects. I saw father, his whole body on top of mother, sobbing and weeping. As soon as the doctor noticed the light, he turned around and said solemnly: "It is not necessary, your mother is alive, she will get better." At that father shot upright and, with open hands like a Christ showing his wounds, he looked with a face full of happiness at mother, who was now calm and sleeping. Great tears leaked from his eyes . . .

It didn't surprise me at all that mother was not dead. Full of reverence I let the sacred candle burn. The flame was now in the dark room, red as a drop of blood, writhing up and down like a soul in torment. The reddish glow of the candle passed across mother's face and made dark shadows in her sunken cheeks, like holes in her head. But then came the lightning, chasing away the candle's glow and trembling across mother's face, so that it was as if her head were being lit from within, like a flame in an alabaster vase. Father was now cheerful and expressed his joy to the doctor, but the latter probably had his thoughts elsewhere, because he did not answer and rustled the pages of a notebook back and forth, so that it made a sound as if there were a bat flapping round the room.

And with the silence that mysterious presence again was felt, as if someone were around us whom we did not see. My heart began to beat hard, a shiver went through me and an indescribable fear of I-know-not-what descended on me. And suddenly the thought flashed on my mind, that it was *my* mother lying there. My mother! . . . Now for the first time the fear of losing her arose in me. I had the assurance that I would lose her, notwithstanding the doctor's statement "She will get better". It became a great pain in me. I wanted to know what was going to happen to her, and my mouth opened to ask the doctor. But I did not dare speak, fearing that he would pronounce her death sentence. I looked at the good woman, suddenly so consciously precious to me, and then I wept . . . The twilight had become darkness, the candle burned more brightly, and its sooty smell was bitter in the mouth. Yet did the light of the candle force its way through mother's emaciated limbs? . . . Did the blessing of the priest, imprinted in the candle, radiate from the flame into her blood? . . . It seemed to me that under the flesh a thin glow was becoming visible.

Was this life returning? . . . She opened her eyes wide and had a good look around the room. She smiled at us as if there had never been anything wrong, with an everyday sweetness like a woman returning from the market. Was she now suddenly cured? . . . A healthy person had never been more splendidly alive! And when she saw the candle, she said: "Why did you do that? . . . I feel perfectly well." I did not see what her face was like when she spoke, because I closed my eyes at the first word in fearful surprise. That voice was a previously unheard, sombre sound: as if it came from Death itself. Oh, never will I forget this mysterious sound! Was that my mother who spoke? . . . Oh, now I had found in one sound the assurance that her soul was already shadowed by the light of the abyss. I wanted to pinch out the flame, but just as sombre a voice sounded: "Leave it, this pleases God." And she smiled at father, who was so overjoyed that all he could say was: "Do you want something to drink?" When she nodded the doctor gave her the cool water, which she just touched with her lips. And while the doctor felt her pulse she said: "All of you go downstairs and eat something. I need rest. Leave me alone." – "Yes, come," said the doctor to us; and to her: "Don't lose heart, the illness will turn." Father laughed doubtfully, as if he could not believe it. But had they not both heard that Death had spoken through mother's mouth? . . . And now I felt the anguish that father must have felt just now when he thought that mother was dead. Oh, that voice, which was no longer hers and sounded as heavy as lead! I can still hear it, hollow as if it came from a barrel. And we went downstairs, after father and I had first pressed a kiss on mother's smooth, taut, white forehead. The stairs creaked beneath our careful steps and in the narrow corridors that criss-crossed the house there lay a tangible chilly silence.

We came into the dark kitchen, which was lit up three times by the lightning that flickered in through the cross-window. Three times I saw the wood outlined against the trembling lit sky like a black cross. Father lit the lamp and soon the cold yellow light shone high on the high white walls, scantily hung with black-framed etchings and portraits, and the sharp shadows of the objects reached up elongated to the ceiling. We gathered around the round dining table, but the light dazzled us and I put a shade over the lamp glass, so that the whole kitchen suddenly stood in a dark velvet twilight. Only on the pinewood table top and on our pale hands did the bright light fall, and on the ceiling was there a swarming sheet of light . . .

Here the doctor would now say whether we should order a coffin for mother, or whether we might still boil up a herb mixture for her. We awaited this momentous news in respectful silence. I could not read the doctor's thoughts from his face, since he was sunk too much in the twilight, but his hands, which lay on the table, were white, with two gold rings. They lay there pure and calm, as if they had had their fill and wished for nothing more. It seemed to me that they were telling us soundlessly what he knew in his head and felt in his heart about mother's life: it was reassuring . . . We said nothing, but after a violent crash of thunder, I saw father's hands moving and his finger lightly scratching the table top. I could see from his hands that he was restless and wanted to ask something. This hesitant feeling of father's about asking a question, which must bring out the truth about his most precious possession, lay so clearly defined in his hands, that since then I have put more trust in hands than human eyes. What for us was a momentous word, which would be the beginning of a great sorrow or of a new hope, had to come from the doctor: a simple man, for whom the subject on which he must give his judgment was indifferent! How strange! . . . Suddenly father's hands leapt up – curiosity which had swollen up and was looking for an outlet – and grasped those of the doctor, and from the darkness in which his mouth was sunk, his voice asked weakly as if stifled by the twilight: "Tell me honestly, will she die? . . ." The doctor's hand went up and a loud roll of thunder drowned out what he said. "What did you say?" Father's mouth quivered, as if he thought that heaven itself wanted to hide the cruel oracle from him, and he squeezed the doctor's hands more nervously. The latter replied convincingly (as a sighted person says to a blind one "It's day" when it is day): "She will recover." And father's hands met and folded together full of gratitude . . . Was this then the last word? The Truth? . . .

I don't know, it came so grudgingly out of his mouth, it sounded so lost in the silent kitchen. It did not reach my expectant heart. Shouldn't I have been glad? . . . Yet I knew that the doctor was judging mother's condition by the apparent improvement. And is Death then no further away from a sickly old man than from a blushing child, picking flowers in the meadow? ... What do we men know of Death? I didn't believe him. The mighty pressure of something unknown, that lay like water on my heart, gave me the assurance that something else was happening to mother ... I did not dare think of what I felt. Oh! it was as if the walls had a breath that went through my soul! My mother was going to die! My mother was perhaps already dead! ... I had wanted to jump up, run upstairs to find out, but it was as if I was as heavy as lead ...

The doctor had now started talking about trivial matters and in that way tried to make his satisfaction clear to my father. I heard them, but what they said I have forgotten.

And since I now saw their hands expressing their deepest feelings, I started thinking about people's hands, despite the fact that I knew that a sombre power was prowling around me; how their behaviour is a clear reflection of people's inner life! And I thought of the hands of the millions of people on earth ... But suddenly the harsh ticking of the pendulum clock dispelled my thoughts and at the same time I heard the pendulum of the mechanism stop, just (I learned later) as it was about to strike half past seven ... When I became aware of this, gooseflesh ran up and down the whole length of my trembling body and the blood froze in my veins, as if my body were pierced with thick barbed wire, which held my limbs taut. Why did the clock stop?

What this a sign that mother's life had stopped? ... The blood suddenly gushed wildly through my body and my heart pounded with a heavy thud like a mallet.

I was very sorry that I had heard the clock stop, here in this house where coincidence was such a precise revelation of the unknown! Neither father nor the doctor had heard and they went on talking . . . What if even now she were dead? . . . I wanted to go and look, be certain, but I could not move, the way one feels when one is having a nightmare. It was as if there was a wind around my face, it was like the breath of someone leaning over my shoulder. Was it my mother's ghost floating around me? Just then father was telling the story of the beggar who drowned in the moat: "Then he fell forward in the dirty water, which soon closed over him. He did not come up again, but his right hand kept sticking out of the water and grasping." Outside I heard a long sigh, as if from a person. It was the wind which had risen, chasing across the plain and howling in the trees. It beat against the door and I heard a handle fall in the corridor. It wailed in the chimney like a madwoman. I thought I would die of fright and the sweat ran from my forehead in great streams. It was as if a sighing approached from the walls; the ground shook; everything seemed to be alive! . . . The thunder rumbled as powerfully as ever and each time the lightning flashed it made a black cross on the window. But didn't father also sense that mother was dead? . . . I would have liked to shout it out, but my throat was as if choked against all sound. And he finished: "Oh, his piercing scream, which we heard as a dying cry and summoned us to the window, did no good. We simply looked at each other in surprise, as if what was happening there were a story. We could so easily have rescued him!" "It is amazing," the doctor replied, "that when Death is really involved, haven't you noticed, that all our power to rescue the dying person is paralysed, that we are as it were hypnotised by I know not what mysterious force, and we are powerless? . . . It is certain that many of our deeds are not ours and that a kind of Divinity sometimes takes our place, which obliges us to let Heaven's will take its course . . ." Then there was again the silence which gave me a pure sense of the presence of something else. I thought I was going crazy with fear and inner tension. Father suddenly said out of politeness: "Before we forget; let's have a glass of wine," and to me: "My boy, fetch us a jug." With his words it was as everything that had strength and courage flowed out of my body. In order to fetch the wine, I had to go into the large front room where several jugs were kept in a heavy oak cupboard. From habit I was able to find everything in the dark. I didn't take a match, so as not to show father that I was afraid. I went down the dark corridor, which was just being lit up by lightning and between the bars of the spyhole in the front door I saw the whiteness of the convent wall ghostly flickering. At the staircase I stopped and listened to upstairs, where it remained deathly still. I had only a few steps to climb to satisfy myself whether mother was dead, but I was like one who, when the truth shows itself, closes his eyes. My heart was wrung with curiosity in my bosom, but I dared not go and look. I had to go on, so as not to fall. The door of the front room creaked and a chokingly dull smell hit me from the dark place as a chilly blast in my sweaty face. I wanted to be bold but I thought I would sink into the ground when I saw two small, light green flames staring at me from above the cupboard.

My hair stood on end from terror and the first sound of a raw scream of fear was already trembling in my mouth, when the lightning flash fell into the room and I recognised in the two flames the eyes of our secretive ginger tomcat. I was angry with myself and went over to pull the creature off the cupboard and gave it a kick, which made it let out such a painful cry that I shuddered. I took the wine and grasped the tomcat, which had crawled into a corner, under my arm . . . When I entered the room, my father had already put out three crystal glasses on the table and in my place was the glass from which my mother always drank. It was round and tulip-shaped, opening up elegantly on a slender stand, with a flat base. Father poured. It saddened me to have to drink from this glass of mother's, which had never been used by anyone but her. Father must have put it out without thinking. No, I wouldn't drink from it. I clinked glasses, but did not drink.

And again father went on telling stories to the doctor. But couldn't they feel that there was a dead person in the house? I would wait to go upstairs and look until they went, but the slow time seemed to last ages. I stifled my sighs and in order to hide my nervousness, I stroked the coat of the skinny tomcat, which was now purring on my lap. I was horrified by clearly feeling his ribs and spine. I suddenly felt such revulsion towards him that I tried to push him away, but he sprang over the table and knocked over my full glass of wine, which crashed down and shattered to pieces. The red wine flowed across the table in a wide puddle and gushed in all directions, reaching the edge of the table and leaking onto the ground in thick drops. I could have wept because this glass had been broken . . .

And now the fear in me became like a blazing fire, which flared up and flushed scorching through my whole body. I felt so full of pain, as if all my limbs were being tortured by a whitlow. I could no longer stand it. And with a raging scream I tried to push away all my fear and imaginings, but the doctor got up, took the shade off the lamp in order to see the time. Again the white kitchen was bathed in the harsh lamplight. "Only seven-thirty," said my father. I did not dare say anything. But when they also heard no sound and saw that the pendulum pointed downwards motionless like an index finger, they realised that the clock had stopped at that time. The doctor looked at his watch which indicated nine. "We'll wait a bit longer," he said, "the thunder is abating, I shall be able to leave shortly." "Shouldn't we go and see mother?" asked father. "Let her rest, it will do her good. The illness has subsided greatly. After good treatment she'll be able to go for a walk on the plain next spring."

Father laughed warmly. It had become unbearable for me. I wanted to be sure, or it would choke me. I was at one of the extremes of human life, where it is no longer possible to remain the same and you must be recreated if you do not want to be struck down by a stroke or by Death. And suddenly, unexpectedly it was there! I still shudder at the thought . . . A cautious ring of the bell sounded in the corridor, another . . . and another. And then a deep silence. They were like three beats of an iron heart. At the same time a strange force entered the house, each of us was aware of it and went pale. Oh, now father and the doctor first became aware of what had been weighing on my heart for so long!

We looked at each other full of fear. Who was at the door so late on that lonely road? I became as cold as ice and my knees knocked. It was as if there were holes in my body, through which all my strength escaped, like water through a sieve. Was it Death itself coming to ring at the front door with its bony presence, to bring us the sad news? . . . Father looked at me, I looked at him and we looked at each other as we never had looked or will look at each other again. We read in our eyes what we both felt. Now he understood and grabbed the doctor with a clawing hand and asked hoarsely and feverishly: "She won't, will she? She won't die?" Had the doctor not heard? Did he not want to answer? . . . All he said was: "Someone is waiting outside, I shall open up," and at the same time he disappeared into the dark corridor. Our souls had opened their eyes!

Father was lying against the wall with his head thrust forward, listening in fearful tension, aware that something terrible was about to come. We heard the doctor open up and then there was a sound of a short whisper, from a strange, deep man's voice. I saw father's mouth open and his eyes grow wider. What was going to approach? Who was there? The time lasted an eternity for me, so that my thoughts charged on like wild flames, piercing as snow in a north wind. I felt as if in this one moment ten lives could elapse.

But the door opened and the doctor let in a tall, pale man. He was dressed in black, with a white tie, a black silk hat and black gloves. His eyes were set very deep in his head and the thin-lipped mouth was closed like a gash in his long pale face. He looked at us with a fixed glance, in which there swam something like sincere pity. Slowly he handed father a white, black-bordered card that had an ordinary name – which I have now forgotten – printed on it with beneath it the word *Mourner*, and as he handed it to father, whose arms hung limply by his sides, he said in a dark, hollow voice: "Deepest condolences. May I pray for the deceased in town?"

Did a man ever go paler at the most horrid event than father and I at those few words? . . . I saw father go pale, rise up and look at the man in desperation, as he cried: "Dead! Dead! . . . She? . . . How do you know that?" But the strange man said very simply, like one who does not know: "I just thought . . . and so . . . But if she's not dead . . ." The doctor interrupted him curtly. "Be quiet, you lout," and said to father, laughing and consoling: "Oh, he's an idiot . . . simple-minded . . . I know him. He's been dreaming again. He talks nonsense to people every day, and turning to the man again, whose tough face now implored pity: "I thought that you had something so serious to say?" But no sooner had I heard the mourner's first words than I felt myself standing in a great blinding light that scorched my soul. I let out a raw cry, for the truth of his words danced like flaming blood before my eyes. It was as if with this clear awareness my body was crawling with a thousand ants. And like a raging animal I ran into the corridor and charged up the stairs to mother! . . .

The candle had almost burnt out, a blue flame still rocked above the liquid wax. With a cry I leapt forward to the white bed, threw my arms round mother's body and pressed my mouth on her forehead. But I shrank back, for her forehead was as cold as ice and her limbs stiff. And then I saw her lying there in the trembling candlelight, white as snow in moonlight, with her mouth wide open and her neck stretched. And the one open eye, in which the candle flame quivered, looked at me coldly and accusingly!

She was dead! . . .'

# THE CELLAR

Walking through a spacious, cool church that had no people in it and where the evening twilight had gathered thickly and silence reigned mysteriously, I found a large envelope, standing out white where it lay on the dark, cold stones.

I picked it up and studied it by the soft light that came through a blue glass window (depicting the life of St Francis) and hesitantly reached the high, silent pillars . . .

The envelope was dirty and greasy from many fingerprints and was closed with five dark-red seals. The address had been written several times, but repeatedly crossed out in black and at the top four stamps had been stuck, which had not been postmarked.

I found all this so mysterious that I could not stop myself from tearing it open . . . There were about ten sheets of fine paper on which tightly spaced lines were written in small cramped letters, so that it hurt the eyes. How my astonishment mounted when on the first page I read '21 July 1885'! The curious urge to find out about this unsent letter flooded so powerfully through my system that I wanted to read it immediately. And in order to see better and not be disturbed, I took my place in a dark side chapel, where a candle thickly covered in wax drippings illuminated a Gothic representation of Our Lady of the Seven Sorrows with a smoking, dancing flame. And in that tremendous, painful clarity, which dripped over the white papers, I read the following:

*Dearly Beloved Friend,*

We have not written each other for a long time. Had we forgotten each other? . . . Perhaps!

But now, now that the most terrible thing in the world has befallen me, it is first and foremost you who loom large in my thoughts and it makes me feel truly happy to be able to inform you of my horrific experience. Perhaps I should not do it, but the sea lies between us and I would be complaining to the dumb, and who better than you can I tell? . . . Promise me to burn this letter! . . .

You know how by nature I was drawn to mysticism, how I could not imagine a human being, an object, deed or force without seeing a soul behind it. This feeling was always fed and nourished by my great number of books, dealing with secret science. Yet among those books there was one in particular that I loved above all. It was called: *This is the key to the dark chamber, which is called the future.* It was a folio manuscript dating from a previous century. From the parchment pages, firmly bound in a black leather volume with seven silver locks, there wafted a warm smell of mouldy antiquity.

My uncle had found it with other sacred books in various languages on a hunting trip to the East Indies, in the hidden cellars of a buried temple, lost and forgotten in the dark forests of the East . . . It had obviously been written under the influence of Indian works. Nevertheless, it testified to profound mystical knowledge and superior existential wisdom. It laid claim to a pure and absolute clairvoyance. It depicted a clear and detailed system of the future of the world and of human beings, and in addition indicated the means for every individual to accelerate that future. Before I proceed I will give you a very concise and incomplete overview of that proposed future.

God is the eternal fire of which our souls are the sparks. He sent us forth into matter, which is his eternal body, and we worked our way up unconsciously in the form of what we now call monades, past the mineral, vegetable and animal realms, until we, having risen to a certain point of development, separated from them as man, which is a self-conscious centre in the universe . . . Yet from the moment our soul penetrated matter, it divided, and one part took place in female form and the other in male form. And those two souls, from in the lowest mineral, vibrate and constantly incline towards each other to regain their broken unity. That is the reason for the urge toward growth in nature. They will always go together in life and death, along the whole length of the thousands of reincarnations and will draw closer and closer together, and one day in the distant future, after the full development of the man and woman, will merge into one soul, which will reign in the form that is neither man nor woman. A few souls, scattered across our earth, already possess that complete unity. But everyone shall and must reach it. Then a new period of life will have dawned for mankind. Man will be more beautiful than we can ever imagine, and so fine and ethereal that it will remain invisible to our present eyes and the densest matter, neither fire nor water, will be an obstacle to it. Then man will possess full knowledge and the mystery will no longer be a mystery. Disasters and accidents will have ceased to exist; thunder and lightning and all the destructive elements of earth and heaven will lie sunk in an eternal sleep. Then people will no longer know what pain is, which only exists through separation. In a word, pure happiness and great peace will go over the world and the time will have come when the gods live among men . . .

And oh, dear friend, I believed and lived with all my heart and soul that teaching which I now curse! . . . On first reading it was as if my heart opened with extreme joy . . . New life entered into me, a peace I had never known. I applied this system down to my most trivial deeds, focused my heart and intellect on everything even remotely connected with it, while remaining strong and hard in opposition to everything outside it . . . I was very strict in the matter of purity in particular, since according to the book purity has the greatest power to waken inner capacities at present stifled by our passions and make them grow beyond the material . . .

For a long time I lived in solitude, burning with longing for the great day, which I knew was still hidden deep in the immeasurable pit of time . . . But gradually there arose unconsciously in me the burning desire to find the woman who bore the soul which one day must merge with mine. I was curious about her. And suddenly, unexpectedly, she was there . . .

Opposite us in a large white mansion there lived an old gentleman with his two nieces, who were young in years and slender in stature. The youngest had seen twenty springs and was as pleasant to look at as corn in the sun. In the blond, delicate oval head, which was gracefully borne upon a tender, slim body and a long white neck, there opened two large, perhaps too large, very dark blue eyes with a bright innocent sheen onto life.

Having outgrown her childhood behind the high walls of an institute for young ladies, she had come to live with her uncle with an ordinary amount of knowledge, but in her heart had brought an ample treasure of golden sounds, which she threw open on the black piano, behind the thickly curtained window, in sense-enchanting chords . . . I saw little of her, but in the evenings – it was summer then and the street was very quiet – I heard her on the serious piano weaving great sound poems with the utmost sensitivity.

In that woman there lived a world of powerful feeling, for like a high silver moon over a sleeping lake, the profound melodies of Beethoven welled on the quiet evening street; like the constantly alternating song of the sea, now sweet and glad as a spring morning, now churning and bubbling with long-borne pain and passion, sank and climbed the titanic song of Wagner.

That woman was hiding a great soul.

And while it was precisely the time when I longed for the soul destined for me and was becoming hopeless at the thought that I might have to go through life alone, it suddenly surprised me that I had never thought of this girl, who was called Mina. That evening she unfurled a slow dreamscape by Chopin and I cried. When I went to bed I was aware that it was she who had accompanied me through the various lives! My soul grew with tangible happiness and it was as if I were drinking the light of the blue mountains! . . . Not an evening went by from then on without my staying by the window, sometimes till late at night, when the white house was already dark and locked up.

She was always accompanied by a maid when she went shopping, and the old gentleman, severe in his three-piece tailcoat, which hung around his shoulders winter and summer, always went with her to walk along the *Sacred Ponds* and the *Béguine Woods*. Those walks were long and pleasant. Soon I went in the same direction, and when I met them, her uncle answered my greeting earnestly, and Mina focused a long, cold look on my eyes . . . Yet I met them so often and must probably have looked at her in such a way that she could read in my eyes what I felt in my heart. For a light came into her eyes that had never been in them before and a silent smile caressed her mouth, which was as soft as a downy fruit. Desire made my soul outgrow me. I felt a new life wafting towards me and my heart swelled with blissful delights . . .

But autumn tossed the leaves into the grey sky which hung low and wept. The cold kept doors shut and winter squeezed the last life to death in its icy arms . . . I no longer saw Mina, but in the evenings her music flowed over the austere house fronts like a summer. And I was happy, felt through everything that something of me had settled in her, and that a silent voice conducted an intimate language between us.

I was like a May, when the sky is blue and the fields green, and the promise of life goes through the earth like a great vibration.

But I was happy in my hope and as I waited felt the roots of the theory of the future, deeper and stronger, full of an urge towards new life, creeping forward in my heart . . .

Our town is an ordinary little provincial town, where it is very quiet and many monasteries erect their austere walls. During the winter I remained deeply absorbed in the study of secret science, and on Sundays I generally drove to the big town to follow the concerts, where classical music was performed superbly. My place was always right up against the ceiling. It is there that artists of all kinds come to listen. One hears the music very purely, and it is more intimate because one cannot see the players and it is almost totally dark . . .

On one of the cold Sundays of the winter in question I had gone to a concert devoted to Beethoven. When I entered the hall – it was very late – they were starting the seventh symphony. A vague, distant, broken light scarcely floated on the heads of the wild-haired artists who, with eyes closed and with their white hands in their beards, sat listening motionless. As I sat down I was not a little alarmed to see Mina sitting next to me accompanied by her uncle and sister. A great shudder of unknown happiness went through me. The distant light that dusted her white open presence with gold was like her soul, which having climbed out of the depths of her being, came to listen. In her large eyes there was a flame of powerful inspiration. While I focused all my attention on Mina and my soul, purified by the music, unfolded like the light in the morning, I boldly moved my hand to hers, which was tender and soft as velvet. Oh! it was as if when I became aware of her flesh I melted with intense happiness! . . . It was as if the life contained in that little hand drove all mine out of me. And slowly her delicate fingers rose and wound around mine, pinching . . . Then my blood surged wildly up, for in this little gesture lay the destiny of two lives that was depicted in unborn days. So, she knew I was sitting next to her and she loved me! Something swelled up in me that brought tears to my eyes. I felt as if I were swimming around in mournful, sweet music, which was like singing water into which I was plunged.

Mina turned her face towards me, and her eyes, in which a hitherto unknown fire blazed, looked at me with motionless admiration. A light flashed from them that penetrated deep within me and illuminated the depths of my heart. And greater and greater they rose, until I saw no more than those two eyes, large as two dark worlds with a flaming soul! . . . It was as if I was bound to die under that look, but suddenly with a roll of thunder in the orchestra the divine Fate burst out, and as if paralysed and broken by its power, she turned her head and let her hand slide from mine. I still think of how at the same moment when our souls wrapped around each other, Fate, symbolised in the music, tore them apart. Unfortunately, the same thing happened in our lives. But at this moment I was at the highest point of happiness in my life; it was as if I were the music itself which now mightily, burning and boiling with happiness, mounted to heaven . . .

Once the poem of sounds had rolled out, frantic clapping burst out from all directions. Suddenly it occurred to me to make use of this occasion to tell Mina that I wished to speak to her. I quickly bent over to her and whispered clearly: 'I'll be waiting for you tomorrow at seven o'clock in Cederstraat . . .' She acted as if she had not heard anything and went on clapping with her small hands. Then she got up and left the hall with her uncle and sister, without giving me so much as a look.

. . . The street where I waited for Mina the next day, and which I had chosen because of its quietness and solitude, began in the shadow of the back of the grey, massive parish church, and consisted on both sides of high white walls, behind which were situated, dark-green, the gardens of two monasteries. These monasteries formed the other part of the street, which turned back at right angles and suddenly ran up against a large deserted house with barred windows and stone walls which were cemented in to those of the monasteries.

This house, where centuries before a king had lived, had been uninhabited for years because of its lonely situation, and so no one went down this dead-end street but the occasional monk or a pair of silent white nuns. To the right of the house was the convent, which was white and high with square multi-paned frosted windows. And the black friars' monastery on the left was built in late-Gothic style, with many fragments of holy sculpture in the dark alcoves. The building, on which time had taken its toll, was dirty and dilapidated as if the weight of the endless days had lain on top of it and caused it to subside. The entrance gates were opposite each other in the middle of the street. Less than two hours' sun shone on the paving stones, between which grass pushed up its green shoots. And over there behind the garden wall of the convent, at the turn of the street, there spread out high and wide a huge cedar tree, which covered the whole sky in black. It stood there mighty and unmoving in its immortal darkness like a silent God that would outlast time and eternity. It was like the watchman, the soul of this street where silence and shadow reigned . . .

Here I waited, walking to and fro. The evening was heavy and dark. A thin mist hung in the air and sweated itself out on the clammy ground. A paraffin lamp in the corner of the convent burned hopelessly a dull, blood-red flame, which glimmered on the wet stones. Now and then from a distance there sounded the silvery chimes of a hasty convent clock, and apart from that everything was as silent as the grave.

Finally, I heard from behind the turning of the street the sound of a rapid, light step.

I went towards the sound and recognised in the weak light of the streetlamp the slender figure of Mina, wrapped in a wide cloak. When I spoke to her my voice trembled with emotion and happiness, and hand in hand we began walking up and down the silent street. I told how my love for her had grown as quickly as a flower and described how it was a sweet pain to me to have borne the burden of that love alone for so long. And she was able to say in a very childlike way how my image was like a beneficent barb in her thoughts, and the pleasure it gave her when she knew that I was listening to her music. Her words, which came from deep in her throat and were sweet and warm as the sound of an oboe in the evening, brought a deep peace to my heart.

Then we strolled silently in the darkness, tasting the new happiness like a juicy fruit. We huddled close together and repeatedly squeezed each other's hands. It was very quiet. But suddenly a double ringing of bells broke loose over us, and behind the windows of the monastery, in which a red glow now shone dimly, a murmuring of many deep male voices arose, muttering evening prayers. And in the white convent, above softly rustling organ peals, there floated the velvety voice of a nun. We were struck by this, and as if moved to ecstasy by this sudden and unexpected beauty we embraced involuntarily. It seemed to me as if with that kiss our souls had opened to each other . . . The tears trembled in my eyes . . . We now spoke about the intimacy, the mysticism that existed in this street, and we arrived in front of the deserted house that rose up huge in its mass of stone in the darkness. We admired its location in this lonely silence, which was harmonically broken by prayer and the voices of bronze bells. We looked with reverence at this house, through which antiquity had passed and where it still trembled like a soul. And together we noticed how this residence was as it were made for us. Both of us carried with us the wish to live there later.

I loved Mina oh so tremendously that my life had become nothing but loving her. And she bore my love like a child carrying a bunch of spring flowers. Gradually I managed to infuse my conversation with my wisdom and philosophy. Mina longed for this and soon I had involved her to such an extent that the two of us were inspired by a single aim: to live in pure love, to speed on our future. Our marriage would therefore be a marriage of souls.

So the winter evenings passed in intimacy in the lonely Cederstraat. We never sought another spot, it was as if we had lost our souls there and could give a voice to our love nowhere else but there.

And that house! that deserted house . . . We dreamed of living there as if our happiness awaited us behind the barred windows and the high door. We could not imagine our future without that house. It seemed as fatally predestined for us as life and death. And it was as if the longing in us to be married hammered and banged only in order to live behind the walls of this mysterious house! . . .

I informed my parents and Mina's uncle of this wish.

And now I visited her at home every evening, where despite the deeply felt music it remained very uncomfortable. Only now did we feel the very special way in which Cederstraat affected us. We regretted the days when we walked to and fro there in the darkness, and now the sharp light of the chandelier clashed around us, revealed shiny frames and glittering objects, and exploded laughing in high mirrors. It was as if our souls only tended towards each other in darkness. And the longing to live in the sombre house in Cederstraat excited and heated us to such a degree that we were to marry sooner than we had intended . . . We were filled with joyful expectation. Yet what a surprise it was when one evening I saw a light burning behind one of the big windows of the house in Cederstraat! The thought that it might be inhabited smashed the dream I had carefully built up to smithereens. Hopelessly, full of haste, I went and told Mina. It was as if something broke in her, and sorrow was visible in her open face.

I hurried to the owner, who was still waiting for a sale and in the meantime was letting two homeless old women live in it. I bought the house and it was as if he cast happiness around me when he put the large rusty keys in my hands . . .

I went to visit the house with Mina. It rose up in massive bluestone, supporting a slate roof from which a large number of chimneys, distempered in white, protruded in an ungainly way.

The many windows, above which early-Renaissance ornaments folded with heavy elegance, were barred with iron bars two fingers thick.

Our hearts stood still when we saw the big door, fitted with a heavy knocker, open with a creak. The house was large and silent, full of old smells. On all sides crisscrossed wide white corridors, which led to the high dark rooms.

The daylight, which crept with difficulty through the green stained-glass windows, trembled here and there with some dying gold on the dark leather stretched along the walls. A high wide chimney sat richly carved above a deep black hearth and carried up to the high ceiling from which iron candelabra hung broadly down, an old painting, in which dimly discernible was a knight with a fierce look.

A wide, slowly turning oak staircase, whose rich carved banisters rested on an amply draped, life-sized statue of a monk, led to the many upstairs chambers, equally dark and silent.

This half-light and the great silence, mixed with the old royal odour, did the soul good. From all the windows at the front of the house, one could see everywhere the monastery and the convent and the dark cedar, immobile, which covered the sky ... Oh, here we were to live, alone with the two of us in this mystical twilight, in which the flame of our pure love would glow like a slender lily! ... We were very happy. Yet it seemed to us strange that under the black and white stones of the corridors and rooms there should be no hidden cellars.

We searched everywhere, down to the room occupied by the old ladies, but to no avail. But behind the house was a garden, of which the few craggy-leafed trees stood out against the dirty white wall of a low ruined house with a red-tiled roof, to which much valerian clung.

This house had two doors and two windows, which were so dusty on the inside that it was impossible to see anything through them. I opened the first door, and in the dark a large hearth loomed up and a cumbersome, broken pump, which immediately told me that this was the kitchen. I then wanted to open the other door, but this had no handle, was firmly locked, and not a single key fitted. Mina was determined to know what that door kept concealed. Then I was able to open the door with a piece of iron, which lay among three very beautiful, moss-covered Romanesque capitals. Dense darkness reigned in this place. I was astonished that there was no ground floor, nothing but a dark depth in which a wide stone staircase wound its way down before our feet. I threw a stone down and from the darkness there sounded to our ears a splash of lots of water. I lit a match and by the scanty light we saw still black water, which filled the whole place . . . It was over two metres deep. This was definitely the cellar. A cellar full of water! Suddenly a shudder went through Mina and she cried in a trembling voice: 'Herman! Oh Herman, I am so frightened of that cellar, close it up, close it up!' I reassured her and laughed at her childish imagination. Nevertheless, she insisted that the cellar be closed again, and she asked this in such a way as if she thought she would die in it. I shivered . . . But the lock was twisted and the door would no longer close. I promised Mina to have the lock fixed in the next few days . . .

Before going we visited the two old ladies again, who sat hunched praying at the window with richly ornamented rosaries. They thanked us for the sum we gave them to move. They promised many prayers for our happiness, as if they, poor in spirit, could ward off the fate that hung over our heads. Alas! . . .

The day of our marriage approached. The old ladies

found a new dwelling, and the house was cleaned and filled with old, dark furniture in the style of the rooms. Tapestries were hung and rugs laid and soon it stood waiting for our love. The next day the sky was overcast and the wind whipped a fine drizzle and reddish leaves across the white town. It was autumn . . . I was as intoxicated by happiness when the blessing of the priest passed over us, and Mina, in her white muslin dress, was matte-pale and carried a white joy in her, which coloured her large blue eyes.

Afterwards there was an intimate gathering of family and friends. Ordinary music and well-known chamber pieces sounded repeatedly. When evening came, falling quickly from the low sky, the wind got up and the rain lashed wildly at the windowpanes.

At ten we had ourselves driven home.

The carriage rolled through the narrow, dark streets, through which the wind blew in sweeps and gusts. It rained constantly as if it were never going to stop, and the few streetlights, dim in the great darkness, poured their weak light into the dirty puddles and on the white gables, behind which everything seemed to be lying dead.

We hastened to be in our room, where I lit a candle in a silver candlestick. The two bedsteads, which stood opposite each other with blue velvet curtains around them, cast large shadows on the gold leather walls. I said something to Mina about the happiness we were now embarked on and then blew out the light, pressed a silent kiss on her brow and each retired to his bed. Now there reigned in the room a heavy darkness, through which the distant streetlamp bored a ghostly, trembling glow, precisely upon a painting depicting St Jerome, who beat his thin chest with a death's head until it bled . . . It was as if the saint were alive and moved in the darkness. The rain beat against the windowpanes and the wind howled and screamed constantly through the bright chimney pipes. Gradually I heard muffled sobs bursting out from behind the velvet curtains. I called out her name.

She did not answer but got out of bed and came to me in her white nightdress, fell on top of me, clamped her hands firmly round my neck and broke into weeping punctuated by rapid sobs. I asked her what was wrong; whether she was afraid of the wind or of the lamplight falling faintly on St Jerome.

In reply to all my questions she went on silently weeping. But after a while she whispered, as if frightened to say it out loud: 'Can't you hear it then? . . . that banging in the night?'

I listened and sure enough, there was a constant pounding that seemed to come from far away and every blow of which thundered through the house like a mighty vibration and could be heard in the night.

In that wild darkness it was frightening to hear. 'What if it came from the cellar?' asked Mina fearfully. I felt myself turning pale at this question. So that mysterious cellar was still haunting her thoughts? . . .

It cut through my heart like a knife. 'I forgot to shut it,' I said involuntarily. 'Come on,' she said, squeezing my body closer to hers, in which her heart was beating like a piece of wood, 'Come on, shut it then, this instant, come on, for I am so afraid.' I lit the candle and saw her face horrible in the reddish glow, her eyes shone large and stupefied and a painful tic drew her bottom lip upwards. She was sallow and beads of sweat covered her forehead. When I saw her like this I hastened to go downstairs. I was very sorry that I had forgotten to shut the cellar. Mina did not dare stay in the bedroom by herself and followed me.

The noise did indeed seem to come from the garden. When I opened the back door, the wind blew out the candle and an impenetrable darkness hung before us. It went on raining the whole time and in the distance a dog howled. We reached the back extension, and very vaguely in the darkness we saw the cellar door open and suddenly close again with a resounding slam.

It was the wind that kept pushing the unlocked door open and shut. I showed Mina how ungrounded her fear was, but she stubbornly wanted the door shut because it was precisely that door.

Unfortunately, I had no means to hand to do this; I could only promise her that it would be closed tomorrow. Downcast, she followed me back to our bedchamber, where I lit two candles, in whose trembling light we lay awake without speaking.

And the wind howled in the flues, beat against the house; the rain lashed against the trembling windowpanes, and on top of it, like a sombre chord, sounded the same pounding of the cellar door. That was our wedding night. After a very long wait the grey morning emerged from the darkness. A pale light began to stir behind the cedar tree, which rose up like a curse against the low sky which did nothing but rain, rained with a sad and sonorous sound . . .

When Mina got up, she looked very exhausted, but her eyes were alive with the glow of innocent joie de vivre . . . Her fear had blown away with the light and when I spoke of closing the cellar, she laughed in shame at her fear and persuaded me that from then on she would be strong. I was pleased to see her borne up by new strength. We visited friends and acquaintances and the night, now without wind and rain, passed calmly.

Before a week had gone by, the two of us were sitting there, as if we had always done so, absorbed in the study of secret science . . .

The autumn was calm, full of milky-pale mists, in which the red of the trees blazed up as the last passion of a dying life . . . Love arched above us like a rich grape-vine.

We were happy. We felt new life bubbling up in us that quickly grew and was as strong as an oak . . . The promise of purity, strictly followed, sometimes brought me such an ineffably sweet feeling that I shivered with joy. Mina's face was bright as a sunflower.

Oh, my wife felt so deeply in those days, so deep and so true! But she was too childlike, too feminine to express her emotion in words, though the black grand piano sent clouds of rejoicing notes through the rooms and bright corridors, as the voice of a golden heart. When I opened to her the high wisdom of my rare books, she came to lay her blond head on my neck and listened in silence, observing me reverently with her beautiful eyes.

And when she felt inwardly the clarity and truth of my words, when the string of her thought vibrated in harmony with my words, she placed a long, light kiss on my mouth. Because she was simple, my wife, as a daisy. She hid nothing in herself. Her soul lay naked on her face. As I saw Mina, that is how she was. With me she was like a dog that loves its master deeply.

She followed me from one place to the other, always

pushing close up against me and only calm when her head was resting on my shoulder. She was devoted to me! For example, it was her greatest joy, after we had spent all day poring over parchment books, to sit hand in hand by the window in the twilight, aimlessly silent, looking at the silent fronts of the monastery and convent and the cedar tree, until the room was full of darkness.

Our souls flowed together like liquids, for this was the greatest joy that Mina gave: the knowledge that half of my soul was living in her. What else was my task in life but to unite the two souls into one, which would then feel the utmost happiness and the highest knowledge burning in itself? . . .

Oh, for the future, which was my only goal, I could write entire pages and sit thinking about them for hours with a smile on my mouth. But this meant – I feel it now for the first time – that I loved myself in Mina and loved her for myself. For I had married her and was living with her for my own happiness, my own pleasure, that the distant future would bring me.

She was the means that must realise my goal. And allowing myself to be absorbed by the highest selfishness, I did not notice the change that was gradually taking place in Mina. But the first indication was some two months after our marriage, one Sunday afternoon.

We were sitting at the window. The twilight weighed on the heavy oak cupboards and trembled in the empty Cederstraat like myriads of whirling crosses. In the hearth a quiet wood fire slowly burned a dead glow on the gold leather and on the tops of the Delft vases on the cupboards.

Mina sat opposite me on a dark cream-yellow cushion. Her dress was pale blue above which her head glowed matte white and dull gold. Her eyes looked silently at me. I had the voluminous book *The Key to the Dark Chamber Called the Future* open on my knees and was reading aloud about purity.

My words, in which I took a gentle pleasure because of the truth with which they were entwined, sounded slow and quiet as if muffled by the twilight. On the tower the evening bell rang. The heavy bronze booming was like a soft bed on which my words sank down. I read:

*Purity is the flower in which the fruit of the only and perfect peace is contained. It is the key to the door that separates two souls from each other. Cultivate it, o pupil, water it with moderation and solitude, for without them thou shalt not be able to walk the path that ends at the feet of eternal happiness.*

*And the great enemy of purity is not the body, but it is those unclean thoughts that stimulate that body and make it tremble for the impure. Resist therefore those impure thoughts before they overwhelm thee. If they come and tempt thee, send them away. Be on thy guard, for they come as wolves in sheep's clothing. For if thou show them respect and they take root and grow in thee, know that they will overwhelm thee and kill thee. Be on thy guard, o pupil, do not tolerate even the approach of their shadow. For it will grow, increase in size and strength and then thy essence will sink in that essence of darkness.*

*O pupil, before that mystical power joins thee with thy soul so as to become two flames and one fire, thou must have the capacity to defeat that false body, that is the desire in thee, at will.*

*For purity will cause to arise in thee a power which*

*everything that is on the earth and in the firmament shall obey and thou shalt see the secrets of great nature open before thee, down to its deepest depths, o pupil.*

I fell silent and looked up at my quiet wife to see whether on hearing those holy words she also felt such a blissful feeling surging through her; but instead of two dark eyes looking at me with inspiration, I saw two fair hands holding a white handkerchief over her face, in which she hid hollow sobs. I was astonished and lifted her hands away. Mina's eyes were glistening with tears.

In reply to all my questions as to what had suddenly taken hold of her, she looked at me sweetly and reproachfully. Those tearful eyes, in which I had always seen a fire of joyful pleasure, alarmed me. I begged her to reveal her hidden grief to me, but she hid her head in her arms and was silent. Then I commanded her.

She rose meekly out of the dark cream-yellow chair, looked at me from head to toe, as if she could not believe it was me who was standing in front of her, and with a great sigh she fell on my shoulder and burst into sobbing tears.

I let her continue, waiting patiently for her reply. She felt that.

After a while she slowly raised her head, which the glow of the hearth caressed with a gentle fire. She looked at me for a long time entreatingly, while the tears ran down her cheeks, trembling to her mouth, and then came pleadingly over her lips: 'Herman, are we always going to live like this?' and without waiting for an answer fell back weeping into the chair.

It was as if a flash of lightning had torn out a piece of my heart! I was shattered by this bearing of her soul, felt a tremor passing through my body and collapsed into a chair like a broken man. A cry forced its way into my throat! But I wanted to control myself and while Mina sat there in the chair in front of me sobbing, I began with a pretence of calm to consider why this destructive statement had risen in her.

And what did I find, naïve as I was? Only that I was imprinting the higher Wisdom too much via the intellect, instead of via the heart. And then I felt my error and said to her that I would no longer elucidate with her the obscure points of Wisdom, that we would no longer work together at the study of holy Wisdom, which was anyway too difficult for a girl's head, but that I would make her 'feel' the sublimity of the inner life through works of art, books, pictures, music, poetry, walks, etc.

She looked at me with a great sigh, then approved my words with a nod of the head, while her eyes were focused on a vague point. She let out another bitter sigh, and as if in stubborn submission she stood up and leant against the hearth, peering into the tiny flames.

Despite all my suffering I was content because I now knew how to take her with me to the high regions of Light and in her rather wilful attitude I saw only a little resentment because I had not understood her previously.

I closed the book, lit the candles in the iron candelabra, poked the fire, and to restore the intimate atmosphere between us, I asked Mina to make some music. She filled that evening with painful songs, which quivered with sorrow borne alone for too long.

For the next few days I studied alone and when I spoke to Mina about mysticism, it was in very lighthearted terms. Whereas we previously stayed up late in the study, I now spent the evenings with her in the living room, unless I was consumed with desire to absorb myself in the books. I made every effort to cheer her up a little, bought her many beautiful collections of poetry, essays and stories, presented her with beautiful pictures, introduced her to my friends and acquaintances and walked with her through the autumn fields which were full of mist and rotting leaves. Although it caused me deep pain that we could no longer explore together the higher concepts of Wisdom, it remained a consolation to know that she and I were seeking the same goal and both felt in us an impulse towards the unification of our souls. For I was assured of the purity of my wife. But a bitter line had appeared around her mouth which never again went away.

What seemed to me strange, however, in her depression, which she attributed to the melancholy autumn weather, was that she, who otherwise let her head lie still on my shoulder, now fell passionately about my neck and started stroking me and kissing me, while her eyes, burning with strange desires, shone so brightly that it often made me afraid. It astonished me that her mouth always retained that bitter line and turned only with difficulty into a smile when I looked at her.

Some days afterwards in the evening I was sitting in my study, which was situated on the first floor at the front. Through three windows, the central one of which had an iron balcony, which bore the coat-of-arms of the former king, I had in daytime a clear view of the monastery and convent and the cedar tree.

In the spacious chamber lined with gold leather there was nothing but a long table with a green rug on it, a few heavy oak chairs and a large dark cupboard in which my books were carefully arranged. Sitting there, reading my books, was my life! But now that Mina no longer came there, there was a tangible emptiness. Again I had seen her so sad that day that I was thoroughly disturbed and could not read . . . She was downstairs, but I could not hear her. I thought of her and a lively feeling of pity arose in me, so that I could no longer stay sitting and I went down to cheer her up.

It was dark in the dining room; the fire in the hearth glowed blood-red and dim among the extinguished coals like the red of the sun behind October clouds. Mina was sitting at the window and looking into the dark lonely street which was strangely lit by the single reddish lantern flame. I sat down next to her, took her hand, which was cold, in mine and asked how it was going.

I felt a shiver go through her. She turned her head and looked straight at me. And again I saw those eyes, as I had once seen them in the theatre, when Fate broke loose in the orchestra.

Again I saw them rise and finally grow big as worlds, but now a light emanated from them, as from the eyes of a cat. She surveyed me for a long time. It made me feel uncomfortable, and to make the look stop, I asked her: 'Mina, what's wrong?'

'Oh! . . .' she cried sighing, suddenly jumped on me, threw her arms round my neck and pulled me towards her with masculine strength, began to kiss me, my eyes, mouth and ears, on my forehead, chin and neck, pressing her head against mine, in wild rapture.

Suddenly the truth hit me on the head like a stone. My wife was sensual. I tore her off me and she fell like a broken woman onto a chair, crying loudly. She did not dare look up, sensing that I had guessed. It was as if my heart had been kicked out of my body, for suddenly I saw all my happiness, my love, life, and future collapse. I felt acutely the futility of our marriage, the mistake I had made by taking her as my wife.

I could have smashed her head in. But I thought of my books which had taught me that the most dreadful circumstances could only be overcome with calm. My fists were trembling ready to strike, my blood was boiling fiercely in my body, and I had to go away to avoid an accident. But as I slammed the door closed behind me, I heard a piercing cry and dull thud coming from the room. I walked back, and in the centre of the chamber Mina lay on the ground, arms outstretched like a crucified Christ, howling like an animal.

I helped her up and threatened to leave her. I emphasised my words, which I intended to realise, I cried so loud and hard that it echoed through the corridors and she crept towards me like a dog about to be beaten.

And she begged so full of submissiveness: 'Forgive me, forgive me! . . .' that I softened and regretted my rapid excitement. I took her up, held her trembling body very, very close to me and gave her to understand through sweet and quiet words that we could not and must not allow ourselves to be persuaded to indulge in that kind of love. I quoted passages from the Holy Books, portrayed to her the nobility of our life and promised her the reward that awaited us.

She did not say a word and went on crying, but when we went to bed she fell about my neck and cried: 'Herman, I shall never do it again.' And that had come from her mouth so convincingly, with such deep remorse, that I felt certain I would never see anything like it again. I cried for the recovered happiness . . .

In the next few days, which now belonged to the winter, Mina had calmed down again, as if that crisis had already driven a lot of excitement and passion out of her. She now seemed to control a mighty will; there was a determined expression in her face and in her actions; but the pain shone greater still in her eyes and around her closed mouth. Never again did she come and sit close to me or kiss me and take my hands in hers. I was glad. I thought I saw her enriched with new strength, a sense-controlling strength. That silent sadness, however, I wanted to extinguish in her. And so I tried everything to cheer her up. I asked my friends, who since I had been married had visited me only one or two times, not to break off our friendship altogether. They came. They were mostly artists, painters, and poets, but their seriousness and passion for art that shone through everything upset Mina still more. She felt hatred and pity for those people, who seemed to live as if in a dream and did not feel life beating powerfully through their hearts like their blood. They saw that their conversations bored Mina and soon they stayed away . . .

Around that time my friend Nand, a poet, came back from a holiday in Spain. He was a big, full-blooded chap, who had unusual gifts and would have become a great man had he wanted to develop them. But he was too inconstant and weak in character. He could go to inns and balls like a normal person, and then spend days shut away like a hermit writing poetry. He liked long poems with a deeply mystical undertone, many beautiful examples of which he began, but never finished a single one. Not consumed by the passion for art, he lived his days with a smile on his red, clean-shaven face, above which lay a thick mess of blond hair. What particularly attracted me to him was his predisposition for secret Science . . .

He was the only one for whom I opened my books, which he studied seriously and eagerly, but whose wisdom he could not experience because the world was still pulling him down too much. Now I had my own home and he still felt the greatest affection for me; we were soon hard at work together in my study.

Nand came from morning till evening, ate and drank with us and what he said brought a smile back to Mina's mouth. For he was witty by nature, was able to mix subtle quips in his conversation, could talk very entertainingly about his many distant journeys, and also had a round, full tenor voice, with which he sang all the best-known opera fragments. Nand really brought joy into the house. Mina liked him greatly. And I liked to see how pleased she was when he came in, for I had not the least suspicion about her love and faithfulness.

So I was happy because Mina was. It was a pleasure for me, sitting upstairs, to hear her pure laughter resound or hear Nand sing some aria or other, among which she was able liberally to scatter light chords like wafting rose petals.

She copied Nand's poems out and meanwhile also conceived a feeling, a passion for writing poetry.

Nand helped her and together they could sit downstairs for hours on end, while I sat in ecstasy upstairs and my soul could not get enough of Holy Wisdom.

So the days passed. It froze heavily and the world was plumed in thick-flaked snow. Everything was white, but the cedar tree remained standing black and dark as if it did not count in the days and belonged outside time and earth. The fires blazed under the dark chimney mantels and Nand, who had again laid aside the reading of the Holy Books, had begun a long poem with Mina. There were still frequent arguments between him and me about concepts of Wisdom and facts, but the great impulse to go into it more deeply had left him.

I saw his inconsistency, in which he repeatedly believed he had the right end of the stick, with a mixture of scorn and pity, because I knew that once again it would not last very long. . . .

With me Mina had become the sort of woman who carries the love for her husband only silently and in her heart. She never laid her head on my shoulder anymore, her lips never plucked a kiss from my mouth. And that gave me a great feeling of peace, since I imagined she was now passionless, and I thought I felt her love wafting around me like the scent of white cloves.

At night I had beautiful dreams, which took me to the antechamber of the double life, while Mina constantly complained of sombre, unpleasant nightmares. Then a night came when a raging wind had got up which seemed to raise the house in the air. The chimneys seemed full of hungrily lowing animals and through the house thudded the hollow sound of the banging cellar door. Mina was sleeping peacefully and her breaths were deep and long. Frightened that Mina would wake, I lay in the dark looking at the vaguely lit image of St Jerome. She went on sleeping. But at the first light of dawn, when the wind had fortunately fallen she came over to me, eyes shining with fear: 'Oh Herman, I can scarcely believe that I'm still alive! All night I've been dreaming that someone had locked me in a coffin, in which I had died; you came and knocked on it, knocked, constantly knocked, like with the cellar door the first night, you wanted to bring me to life in that way, and I heard it, but couldn't come to life! . . .'

I trembled at her quavering words. I did not tell her of course that the knocking that she had heard in her dream was that of the cellar door. I thought it advisable to lock the cellar during her absence, since otherwise she would never be able to overcome her premonition. That day however she stayed at home with Nand, continuing work on the poem . . . Yet I had the feeling that it was not progressing too well, because from downstairs there came nothing but laughter, animated conversation, and light music.

That upset me greatly, because Mina was losing much of her seriousness, she couldn't hide it from me, although she tried her best. I sometimes found her reading books of a fairly light variety; she always managed to avoid my clear discussions of secret science, and when I discussed it with Nand, she lay in a chair, sighing and sometimes yawning with boredom. In the beginning I had hoped that Nand, by rousing her from her grief, would have gradually led her back towards mysticism, but it was completely the opposite, and it came to the point where she lost all interest. I would happily have removed Nand from the house, but I knew that in so doing I would pierce Mina's heart and she would sink even further. Because she liked Nand greatly, not for himself, I thought, but because of the joie de vivre he brought her. So again a few days passed away into oblivion, bringing little joy and a great deal of suffering . . .

A week later . . . The fire crackled red in the dark hearth and a salutary warmth filled my study. I walked back and forth, completely upset by Mina's behaviour and attitude. Outside there was a sharp frost, dusk was quickly falling, and the silent street was grey. The sun was dying red behind the earth. Its light burnt on the top part of the white convent; it bathed the silent cedar tree in a dark flame, floated into my room through a window, touched my hands and wiped a bright caress over the dull gold leather. It was as if behind the street the whole world was alight. Suddenly it occurred to me that all this red presaged wind . . . Tonight it would again push open the cellar door and suck it shut, with formidable crashing and banging . . . I thought of the terror that would seize Mina and so decided to close the cellar door forever. I had seen Mina go out with Nand; so it was now or never that I had the opportunity to act . . . I looked for the necessary tools and went down the steps with them to the cellar.

Before banging a nail into the door, I looked once more at the mysterious depths which worked so harshly on Mina's weak thoughts. Something gold glinted on the top step, I went over to it and picked up the gold heart from Mina's necklace . . . I had seen it glittering on her breast two days before in the red blaze of the open fire . . . I couldn't make head or tail of it and with the intention of asking Mina herself for an explanation, I put the heart in my purse and closed the door with two sturdy nails and lots of strong wire. I thought my work was clumsy and primitive, but it would nevertheless prevent the hollow slamming of the door.

As soon as Mina came home that evening I asked her about the golden heart. She went pale and stuttered indistinct words, while her eyes remained fixed on me with a fearful look . . .

When I asked her: 'Didn't you perhaps lose it in the cellar?' she drew herself up to her full height and said hastily, emphasising every word: 'I've not been there, Herman, what would I do there? . . .'

This made my astonishment great. I showed her the heart and said that I had just found it in the cellar.

She started in terror and a deep blush crept towards her white mother of pearl forehead, radiating over her cheeks; and her broad white eyelids rose like precious shells over her dark eyes, and she said nothing. I observed that this heart definitely had not found its own way to that place. Suddenly she skipped out of her embarrassment and cried out with laughter: 'Yes, I remember, yesterday I popped down to the cellar . . .' and again her eyes were directed at the toes of my shoes.

It seemed strange to me that she had first lied and gone pale and red over such an insignificant event, she who was always so frank. I asked her why on earth she was so anxious about this confession and then she said entreatingly: 'Oh, I didn't dare, because I was afraid it would have displeased you . . .' I believed her, although her attitude was greatly in conflict with what she said. And found the whole thing so childish and ridiculous that half an hour later I had forgotten all about it . . .

If I no longer saw as feasible the growing of our souls towards Unity, I still hoped that Mina would feel revived in her the longing for the full experience of mysticism.

Winter closed in filthily, the sleet filled the streets with mud and the gutters whined day and night their monotonous dirge. A strange cold shivered through the air. The hearths burned in the inhabited rooms and the others remained closed, filled with a clammy chill and a mouldy smell . . .

Suddenly a heavy sadness had descended on Mina,

which made me anxious and of which I could not force her, for all my begging, to tell me the reason. The bright smile had twisted into a bitter line and the pure, crystal-clear voice had lowered to a darker major key; tears sometimes trembled in her eyes and the piano remained closed like a coffin.

Even Nand's visits did not lighten Mina's mood. It surprised me that he himself was withdrawn and had lost much of his jollity. He came regularly, but it was as if his song were stifled in his throat. Downstairs there was always a silence as in a house without people; only when I joined them did both of their faces adopt a mask suggesting forced gaiety. I began to find it strange. I could not believe that they were seriously engaged in writing poetry, because the books remained closed and the papers undisturbed.

What were they up to so silently downstairs? . . . I was not suspicious, but their strange behaviour became a constant torment to me.

On one of those days I was sitting upstairs and since I could no longer hear them move, I was so seized by curiosity that I went downstairs secretly, so as to find out at once the full truth of their covert behaviour . . .

When I threw open the door, Nand was sitting near the window in the red armchair looking full of pity at Mina, who was sobbing with her head resting on the table . . . Both started in fright and Mina tried immediately to wipe away her tears. I asked what was going on. Mina said nothing and Nand, recovered from my unforeseen entrance, said with a casual gesture and great fluency: 'Nothing can be done to help Mina but to go to the South of France.'

'Why?' I asked full of trepidation.

'Because this air is choking her,' said Nand, 'because she needs light and sun, because she has a nervous illness,' and he quickly added: 'She didn't dare tell you, for fear that it would make you suffer. She admitted it to me quite some time ago, and all my attempts to cheer her up, as you see, were to no avail.'

Though believing him, I still asked: 'Is it true, Mina? Are you suffering so much?'

She just shook her head and started crying again. I sat alongside her full of concern and promised to consent to her wish, but said also that we must first call in the doctor, and he might be able to help her with a simpler and less costly remedy. Yet no sooner had I said this than she cried out that she did not want a doctor, that he would discourage her from travelling in order to pocket the money himself, and many other stubborn objections. And suddenly it became clear to me that her sickness was nothing but the feeling of an emptiness in herself, which issued from her idle life, and that her soul was again longing for the precious food of Wisdom. I explained the situation to her and then quoted, in order to support my words, an excerpt from *The Book of the Future*:

*If thou, o Pupil, perceive in thyself a hollowness that thou carriest around everywhere with thee and canst not fill up through intoxication of the senses; if thou art no longer attracted by the things around thee.*

*Know then, o pupil, that thy soul is rising above that lower substance in thyself, that thou art on the threshold of that gate that opens onto the path of Great Peace; that the eve of eternal summer has begun. Bear then that dark emptiness without despair, so that thou canst let that divine spark that slumbers in thy soul blaze up into the fire that extinguishes stars, for then the time will have come.*

Both were silent and dejected. Nand contemplated the ash of his cigarette for a while and then said: 'But supposing it really is a longing for sun?'

I interrupted him and said: 'Then we can await with hope the spring which is on its way.'

A deep silence ensued. I wanted to break it and told them a few things about this circumstance that we are obliged to regard as a joyful fact, which I really did. They said nothing! . . . Nand left earlier than usual and the following day he did not come at all. Mina stayed downstairs all day. I considered it best to leave her alone now, since I knew that the soul speaks best in solitude. Only when it began to grow dark did she come in search of me. She stayed next to me and nestled her golden head against mine. It astonished me greatly, she who had not even taken my hand since the last scene!

I asked what was wrong. 'Nothing,' she said, somewhat embarrassed, 'oh nothing'; and her soft mouth kissed me like a caressing feather . . .

I felt sorry for her, and yet I was glad, since as the book said, I believed I knew she was on the eve of a summer of the soul full of trembling light and sunny warmth. That is why I let her have her way. She kissed me repeatedly on the cheeks while she ran the fingers of one hand through my hair. It was if her own kisses intoxicated her. She held me closer, kissed me on the mouth with wet lips and soon, swift and light as a young cat, she was sitting on my lap. Her caresses became rougher. It surprised me greatly. I felt the blood rushing to my head at the thought that she again felt the former strange glow burning inside her. And for fear of possessing that certainty, I told her I wanted to go on working.

Always meekly obedient, she slid disappointed off my lap and sat down opposite me, supporting her bare elbows on the table, and her blond head, on which the glow of the candelabra swam down as in golden water, rested in her white hands. She remained looking at me with her deep blue eyes in which a feverish light teemed. Her bosom heaved. I pretended to read, but I could not, since I felt that that wild nature, which I thought I had overcome, was again springing up. It made me feel oppressed, and I did not sleep that night . . .

After a few days Nand had a card delivered in which he announced that he had been called to Amsterdam for a long period for unforeseen and urgent reasons.

I was sorry, as he was after all a good friend. It surprised me not a little that Mina, when I talked to her about it, replied, while her eyes, wide with admiration, gazed at me: 'I prefer there to be just the two of us,' and she did not talk about him anymore.

She constantly wanted to be with me now, full of love, caresses, and stroking and did not leave me alone for a moment. She left the piano untouched and when I asked her not to enter my study, she walked through the white corridors and cold rooms.

I often surprised her, wiping clear tears away with her little finger and letting out hollow sighs, and soon I realised that her sickness was not a longing of the soul, but a resurgence of desire.

But while her earlier behaviour was a true welling up of the heart, a transience in life, there seemed to be something artificial and wilful in her professions of love, which made me suspect that she was hiding something, was keeping a secret concealed in herself.

It was in the look in her eyes, and it trembled through her whole being. I was dying to know what it was, but she gave nothing away.

Finally, I became impatient and ordered her explicitly and roughly to say what was on her mind.

She first looked at me for a long time with fearful respect. It happened in the bedroom. The cold morning caressed her face palely.

Then I suddenly saw how thin she had become, how her cheekbones protruded and how the blue shadow lay on her dull, sunken cheeks.

A trembling passed over her lips, she swallowed a few words, and suddenly, like someone submitting totally to God's mercy, she raised her head frankly, shaped her fingers into claws and cried defiantly, full of rage and reproach: 'But can't you feel what I want? Can't you see Death here, going through the dark room? Can't you see what I want? . . . you who married me? . . . who are closest to me, who maintain you live in and through me . . . and you don't even feel it or see it! . . . But can't you see that there's something missing? . . . Can't you feel that there must first be a child before I can be happy? . . .'

I sprang back in dismay, not believing that it was Mina who had screamed these cutting words. She saw how upset I was, made use of it and cried more hoarsely: 'I want to be like any other woman! I too want to fulfil my vocation! I too want to be happy!'

I felt my blood sinking. I had never seen her like this.

I dismissed the rage that was seething in me, tried to be calm and then said to her with great emphasis that she could never expect that of me. My words broke her . . . She cried in her lap, sobbing loudly. I stood and watched her with my spirit crushed.

What I regarded as so holy in her, she came with a cry and trampled on so thoroughly that suddenly I felt the disillusion like a bottomless pit. After a while Mina came to me again, and now that she had revealed her secret longing there was a calm in her and she begged me sobbing: 'Oh, I shall be so happy and thank you and love you eternally. Then we shall be able to lead the same life as before and we shall have gained happiness, Herman! . . .'

The tears flowed quickly and abundantly over her cheeks and leaked onto her pink peignoir, where they gathered darkly, and hollow sobs caught repeatedly in her throat.

I felt great pity and contempt for her longing to be a mother. I explained to her yet again, in quiet, non-hurtful words, the aim and meaning of our lives. But she went on begging. Not a single day, not a single moment were we alone together without her repeating the same question in tears. Yet since she did not resort to crudeness I let her do as she wanted. For I felt rock solid in my theory, so aware of my strength that I looked down at that temptation with a certain pleasure.

I must have been made of iron not to give in, for Mina suffered greatly. She was consumed by her desire and was losing weight visibly. The beautiful deep-blue eyes withdrew deeper below her forehead. Her upper lip lost its undulating form and pulled the nostrils downwards. The skin was stretched over the spools of her fingers, and they shone yellow; and her Adam's apple, hard-boned and pointed, was sharply outlined under the chin . . . She scarcely touched her food anymore, and I often saw her kneeling, praying, weeping. And she never stopped repeating her question.

It became so bad that I forbade her to enter my study, in which I shut myself up to get away from her because I could not study anymore. My heart was full of pain and anxious expectation because I saw my wife gradually dying. Yet there was no battle in myself about giving in. I saw in the whole affair nothing but a test of God, who wanted to try my strength.

Again, like the victim of a shipwreck holding onto a piece of wood, she had clung to my neck and begged and wept more than ever that I would be making her happy. I had fled upstairs, where I lit a candle in a brass candlestick and wanted to submerge my thoughts in reflecting on the *Book of the Future*.

But it did not work. I thought of Mina. The fire in the hearth had burnt to pale ash, and it was chilly in the room.

I heard Mina come upstairs and enter her bedroom. Then the pain welled up so powerfully that I burst into tears . . .

A little later I was woken by the opening of the door; I looked up. It was Mina.

She stood there as if turned to stone and looked straight at me with a dark, cold expression. I asked calmly what she wanted. She remained looking at me for a while without moving, and then suddenly, despairingly, she bared her shoulders.

I recoiled, both because of her shocking act and because of the revulsion the ugliness of her emaciated body caused me.

And before I could open my mouth to cry out, she threw her cold, thin arms around my body and hugged me to her, as if trying to stifle me.

My body felt the rapid pounding of her heart, her panting breath blew in clouds into my cold face, and her eyes again shone like those of a cat in the dark.

I closed my eyes. It was as if the earth were sinking under my feet. I pushed her away full of horror and rage and threw her out of the room. I fell on the table weeping, for now I knew that my wife only wanted a child out of sensuality, and at the same time I felt the bond between us, which had been stretched for so long, breaking; or rather, I felt that there had only ever been a bond between her and me in imagination . . .

The door opened again and through the trembling of my tears I saw her again, one hand making a fist held in front of her, the other hidden behind her back. She hissed sharply at me: 'I can't go on living like this!' And she went off, full of a cruel intention. I hurried after her, and in the bedroom saw her rise up pale in the dark with her hand grasping a revolver, which was white in the hesitant light of the distant streetlamp.

I leapt towards her, and with a great deal of force pulled the weapon away from her. Mina collapsed like a limp rag. I sat her up straight; her flesh was trembling and ice-cold and clammy with sweat. She had scarcely felt me when she grabbed me again, screeching: 'But you're made of stone!' Then I hit her in the face, so that she bounced against the wall; she did not cry but rose up menacingly, with a formidable light in her eyes. I expected the most terrible consequences, but when she saw my direct, wild and contemptuous look, she changed as if by magic and to my great astonishment she said calmly, as if all that had happened meant nothing: 'Herman, I shall try to forget it.' A stream of joy went through me. I immediately thought – to think that I could have been so naïve! – that my strength had triumphed and that the urge to fight had died in her. For her words sounded genuine and full of conviction. I kissed her cold, naked shoulders. I thought I once again possessed Mina in all her unconscious beauty, which had suffered severely, but was not contaminated . . . And the following day she was so truly friendly and calm as if nothing had happened . . .

Two days later I had to go to a distant village to collect an old book of magic, *The Black Ambrosius*. I knew it was in the possession of a farmer who was dying. This book has a wonderful power, and there is a lot to learn from it for those concerned with mysticism . . . The fields lay fallow and here and there were covered with patches of snow, and the only green that one saw was that of thick-headed cabbages. The land had distant panoramas now the trees were bare. The lonely farms lay hunched together in that vastness like dying things. A grey, motionless sky hung stretched over that dead world like a stone mass. It was very cold . . . I was very happy.

On the way back, fine snow was falling which, whipped up by a newly risen sharp north wind, lay over the fields like white ribbons. I kept the precious book hidden in the deep pocket of my overcoat and under my arm I carried in a grey piece of paper a bunch of mandragora plants, which spread a filthy, breathtaking stench. I had bought them from the farmer for their rarity, since I had no use for them . . .

When I got home I went straight to the back of the house to put the mandragora plants in the garden because of their unpleasant smell. But imagine my surprise when I saw the cellar standing open! . . . I had shut that door! I went over and saw that the nails and wire had vanished from the wall and door. They were lying on the ground, alongside the gothic capitals, and at the same time I saw that there were only two capitals lying there. And the day before I had seen three. I immediately went inside to ask Mina for an explanation. The living room was empty and the fire was out. I went upstairs.

Mina was lying in bed, with a withdrawn, waxen face, as if after many days of pain; she looked at me with dull eyes that begged for pity, and with difficulty she said in a friendly tone: 'Herman'. Then she told me hastily, before I could ask anything, that she did not want to be frightened anymore and so had broken open the cellar. Then she had fallen and hurt her back. 'And the Romanesque capital,' I suddenly asked, 'did you get rid of that too?' She gave a scream of terror. This surprised me. She kept looking at me with fear and then answered, hunting for words like one who is lying: 'That . . . that I threw . . . I threw it in . . .' She kept looking at me anxiously, as if expecting something terrible from me. 'Come, come,' I said, 'don't be afraid I'll be angry about that . . . but why did you do it?' 'To . . . to find out if there was still water in it,' she said again, just as worried . . . 'I'm sorry,' I said, believing her but finding her action strange. 'I'm sorry because now that one of those stones, which I admittedly neglected, has disappeared, they are very dear to me.' And consoling her I added: 'But that doesn't matter, Mina, I shall have it retrieved.'

But scarcely had I uttered these unmeaning words when a jolt shook her upright and she fell about my neck, begging me: 'O Herman! Please don't do it . . . No, no! Leave that stone where it is, leave it where it is!'

'Why?' I asked, surprised at that pointless fear.

'Because . . . because . . . you must leave it where it is . . . because I don't like people going into that water. Because then I shall be frightened again.'

Her words hurt my ears like flaming coals. I suddenly became frightened that Mina would go mad. And to reassure her I quickly said: 'I shan't have it done, Mina; rest assured. But rest a little now. Shall I get the doctor to come?' A strong force immediately scintillated through her slim body; she sat up and refused obstinately: 'No, no, no doctor; it's not necessary; I'm not ill, I'm already better; do you think I am going to make myself ridiculous? I want to get up.' She was already sliding her thin white legs out from under the sheets to get up. I restrained her because I saw the waxy colour shining through her downy skin and testifying to great weakness.

She only stayed in bed when I promised I would not call the doctor . . . I was fully convinced that something crazy was brooding in my wife.

The scenes of the last few days, and now this opening of the cellar, of which she had always been so afraid; the throwing in of the capital, just to hear the voice of the mysterious water; and in addition her fearful expression and hesitant words strengthened my cruel suspicion . . . My heart swelled with fearful expectation.

Two days later she rose from the bed and resembled a wilted lily. It was as if that simple pain in her back had drained all the blood from her body. Her flesh was blue with pallor, as if transparent, and terror was in her face . . . I was cut through with fierce pain and watched her constantly. I did not even think about continuing my studies; the study remained cold, with closed books.

I was very sad; for was she not my wife, in whom I always saw my spiritual equal, who was suffering and sad to the point of death and threatened with the most appalling sickness? It was as if all life had fled from her; she seemed to be standing outside life, living in a dream. She had become very strange. She could sit for hours with her hands folded over her knees, staring aimlessly ahead.

Her mouth remained closed the whole while, and a word never passed her lips, except when she had to answer me. Then she was alarmed, had to collect her thoughts to be able to remember it was me, laughed bitterly, and, as if to excuse her attitude, she said: 'It's snowing,' or 'It's cold,' and other ordinary things and very soon afterwards fell back into that stubbornly pointed forward gaze. And in the evenings she came and sat close to me, took my hands in hers, and was silent and full of fear . . . She did not seem to feel love for me; it was as if I had been effaced from her thoughts. When I asked what she was thinking about, she closed her eyes painfully and a shiver went through her body. Then she said weakly: 'Nothing . . . what should I think about?'

When her sister sometimes came to visit Mina, she made an effort to be cheerful, played a few chords on the piano, but immediately stopped, as if she did not dare to play on . . . I stayed with her the whole time, told her stories and read to her: relaxing stories, to which she listened only at the beginning. It hurt me not to be able to unveil how and in what way she had got into this terrible state.

When I spoke of a doctor, who would cure her and take away her sadness and fear, she said curtly that she was not sick or afraid and felt very happy, or else begged me not to do it. I could not get any more out of her. So, you can imagine, dear friend, how her suffering cast a burning shadow over me . . . She lost weight terribly, and I had to pray and beg her to eat the lightest meals . . .

Yet gradually I began to notice that she was always listening to something that made her very afraid. She no longer left me for a moment, followed me from one place to another and did not dare for a moment, even during the day, to be alone in one place; and in the evenings she went with me to bolt the door and asked for lots, lots of light. Then she slid close to me and sat with half-open mouth and wide eyes listening anxiously. Sometimes, in the middle of the night, when I woke up, she would be sitting up in bed listening. To all my entreating questions about the reason for her listening, she said coldly: 'Nothing,' and went on listening. And I found that the most terrible thing of all: listening to something that was not there.

The days were an uninterrupted torture for me, my head weighed like a lead block and my heart seemed to be torn apart by despair and impotence . . . But slowly Mina's terror became definitely so great that she could no longer bear it alone, and one evening in the living room, from where we could hear the trilling of the organ in the convent, she said mysteriously: 'But can't you hear it?' She said this so strangely that I started. 'This organ?' I said. 'This organ?' she said. Now she seemed to hear the organ for the first time. 'Oh no, not that, that other thing . . .' I said 'no' and tried, for the umpteenth time, to convince her that there was nothing to hear and that what she thought she heard existed only in her imagination.

The organ fell silent. She said painfully: 'No, no, it

does not exist in my imagination. I hear it like I would hear anything else; I hear it from morning to evening and especially at night. Oh, Herman, it is so cruel, so frightening; it will kill me.' And she wept; she ran her thin hands through her blond hair, so that it fell loosely like a golden waterfall to her waist and covered the whole of her back. Her eyes grew wide and wild, with much white around the dark pupils. 'Come, Mina,' I said soothingly, 'come, calm down, tell me what's on your mind, say what you can hear, you will lighten your fear.' And after a long silence, during which her breast heaved powerfully, she spoke full of mystery, hoarsely, as if with the voice of one about to die: 'I can hear a child screaming.' And she burst into sobs.

Now I knew that her fear was madness, it pierced my heart like a glowing hook. I asked: 'From where do you hear it?' She was surprised at my question and looked at me for a long time. Then she said hesitantly: 'I don't know . . . I really don't know . . . but I hear it everywhere, everywhere . . . listen, just listen . . .' And she thrust her head forward and lifted her right index finger. With a lump in my throat I consoled her, without thinking of the possible effect of my words: 'We'll have it looked into.' Then a scream let loose from her throat and she fell backwards. I picked her up, and we wept together. Her sickness crushed my heart and soul.

I was morally broken; and to spare her even more piercing suffering I did not call in a doctor. But now that she had confessed, her terror had lightened; she sought me out only in the evening, and during the day she walked alone through the rooms and corridors and even walked into the garden, and sometimes stopped in front of the cellar door. She pushed the door open and then remained motionless, looking from a distance into the mysterious depths.

She acted as if she had been forbidden to do this. Only when I wasn't there or she thought I was in the front room did she do it. I always spied on her. And if I came into the garden, or if she knew I was standing at a window, she jumped aside and went on walking or immediately came inside. Her words became short and curt and hatred for me glowed in her eyes.

She blamed me for everything. She said I was a bad person and would later burn in hell; yet in the evening she came close to me, took my hands in hers, and remained like that, silently sitting and listening. I served only as a shield for her fear. And I let her do as she wanted, never admonishing her and always letting her have her way, in the hope of improvement; for when I thought that this could last my whole life, I felt a burning pain within and would have liked to go to the furthest end of the earth. Perhaps she would improve if we moved, but she stubbornly refused to leave the house. I fastened my hopes on the spring, whose blue breath was wafting from beyond the Béguine Woods, and which would bring light . . . It gave me a glimmer of hope that Mina now dared to go through the house alone, yet always with her ears pricked for the cries of children.

It was mainly the cellar that attracted her. Just as she had formerly fled it, she now longed for it. It had become a passion for her, listening to the depths in front of that cellar. She did it now even when I was with her. She neglected her food for it, and it was only the evening that drove her away.

It seemed obvious to me that she heard the child

crying from that cellar. And she became bolder and even went into it. Then I saw her descending the steps and disappearing into the dark. I was alarmed at a possible accident and went after her. I found her sitting listening on the lowest step of the cellar, almost with her feet in the dark water.

And then, for the first time, I asked: 'But what on earth is it that attracts you so in that cellar, that cellar you used to be so frightened of?' And she said boldly: 'Between me and that cellar there is a bond that is stronger than that between you and me.'

And as in a red flash of lightning I saw her dream flare up, full of sombre tragic prophecy. My heart was jerked out of my body and then I took the firm decision to call in a doctor for Mina. It was time.

The next day, the day on which the most terrible thing happened that can ever descend on a human head, I left for the big town to find a doctor. Mina, to whom I pretended I was going out for books, was frightened of staying in the house by herself, and was to wait for me at her uncle's. So I went on my way reassured.

The doctor, who had no time to listen to me, promised to come the next day himself . . .

However, when on the way back I saw the plain through which the fast train sped, extending before me endlessly under a dark sky with a splash of yellow in the west, my heart was seized by a mysterious premonition. I felt myself becoming weak as a woman and I became afraid of I know not what.

I tried to dispel the hitherto unknown emotion by reading a paper, but the letters danced in front of my eyes, and I lost the rein of my thoughts.

The train stopped and I hastened to Mina's uncle. I

asked myself why I was in a hurry; I didn't know why, but nevertheless my step quickened. I wanted to be with her . . . to . . . I didn't know why; to hug her in my arms, I think, to kiss her, to love her. I felt I had never loved her so much as at this moment.

I hurried and was glad to reach Mina's uncle's house, as if by so doing I were blocking a great misfortune. But the words of her uncle fell on my heart like burning coals when he said that Mina had left. I felt as if lead were sinking into my bones, and a sharp fear cut its way upward. I went back to Cederstraat. It was dark; the cedar tree spread blacker and more mysteriously than ever, in the darkness and behind the frosted windows of the convent a reddish light burned. Our house stood there as if shadowed in the past. There was no light in the window.

I was already glad that Mina would not be at home. But the front door was half open! I went in, lit a light and saw her hat and cloak on the coat rack. So she was home! The living room was empty and without a fire. I thought I would burst with fear. I went through the other rooms, hurried upstairs and found everywhere rooms full of shivering cold and silence. I called Mina's name. The echo sounded through the hollow corridors and afterwards the silence weighed even more heavily . . . And then I went to the back of the house, knowing that passion had overcome her terror, and that for that reason she had come home. The cellar door was wide open and showed a full picture of the mysterious square darkness in the white wall. There was no one, not a sound came from the silent darkness . . . And suddenly the thought crashed into my brain that Mina had drowned in the cellar . . . I felt it.

Suddenly I lost all self-control and would have fallen. But the thought that she could still be rescued supported me. I shouted, cried and raged, went up and down the cellar stairs, pulled my hair out in despair and impotence and had to grasp the wall so as not to jump into the mysterious water myself. I was at my wit's end.

Suddenly the bell of the Blackfriars monastery burst loudly and resoundingly into the air. At the same time my thoughts turned to the friars. They could help me rescue her! Without a moment's reflection I went to the monastery and persistently banged the heavy knocker, whose echoes rolled through the distant corridors, until the gate opened a chink and a fat-headed friar, illuminated by a distant light, showed himself.

He looked at me suspiciously and said gruffly, in a deep voice that seemed to come from his feet, 'The friars have just gone to vespers; come back in a little while.' He made as if to close the gate again.

With a powerful shove I threw it wide open, pushed the dumbstruck friar aside, and hurried through the high corridors without knowing where I was headed.

I heard the sound of singing rising in the distance, went in that direction, and saw at the end of a long gallery, in the trembling light of the candles, two dark rows of friars, singing deeply from under their wide black cowls, advancing slowly and solemnly.

At my frantic shouting, with which I filled the corridors, they turned in astonishment and stopped. I shouted through my tears that my wife had fallen into a cellar full of water, that she might still be saved and would they help?

They did not move and, as they stood there darkly, they were like black granite statues, such as one finds on old graves. But I repeated my entreaties, cried out that every moment of waiting was time lost and fell to my knees.

Then a tall friar came forward, having thrown off his cowl to reveal a pale, dark face with a sharp eagle's nose. He asked for an explanation, which I gave with a trembling voice. He ordered the other friars to continue. They got back into rows as if nothing had happened and disappeared singing through two low doors which were closed.

He himself went away, asking me to wait a little. His absence seemed to me to last a multitude of days.

I was seething with impatience and meanwhile saw how the candle was burning all alone and how light swept against the edges of a tall glass window behind which great night lay over the world.

The corridors were wide and still, full of shivering cold. Now and then, as if carried by a wind, vague organ music and muted song reached my ear. Finally the friar, who was probably the abbot, returned with two heavily built brothers. One was carrying a length of rope and a pulley hook, and the other an iron lantern with a dirty red flame . . .

I pointed out to them the suspicious place.

One friar attached the pulley hook to the rope while the other held out the lantern. The light hit the smooth, black, mysterious surface of the water and trembled against the walls, which shone calmly. My heart stood still as if I no longer had one, and the sweat lay ice-cold on my forehead; my legs were shaking . . .

And what I next perceived, dear friend, is impossible for me to describe to you. I will just tell you what I saw. From that you can best decide what I felt . . .

The friar with the rope went and stood on the bottom step and threw the length of rope with the hook attached far out into the water and slowly drew it back in.

This had already been repeated a number of times. Only the lapping of the water broke the painful silence ... Suddenly the friar called out in triumph, with a sound that broke in his throat: 'I can feel something.' We stuck our heads out, full of fearful expectation. The man was pulling something heavy and had to use extra force.

Slowly he pulled in the rope, and O God! Above the black water, like a flower opening, appeared the pale face of Mina ... Oh! I can still see the face over which death had passed. How awful! The great eyelids were closed, the blond hair stuck darkly over the sunken cheeks and the white forehead, and the mouth, which was half-open, was full of water ...

The pulley hook had caught in the blue dress, above the shoulders. The friar now wanted to pull her out quickly, and we were already stretching out our arms to help when suddenly the clothes tore loose and my wife submerged again ...

I gave a cry and shook so with horror that the abbot had to stand me against the wall if I was not to fall. The friar immediately threw out his hooks once more and a moment later said, 'I've got her again' ... And he pulled her in with a lighter hand, so it seemed. But instead of Mina, he pulled up the lost Romanesque capital around which a cord was wound many times. He pulled higher. And what did I see then? O great God! that I should have experienced this! From that cord hung a swollen, prematurely born, naked child, a hand in length! ...

A four-fold scream cut through the darkness, and the lantern smashed on the steps . . .

I fell unconscious.

When I woke up, my wife and the child had been buried!

I cursed my doctrine, burnt all my books and now wander around with the pain of a two-edged red-hot sword in my heart.

Oh friend, come and visit me and console me with your faith!

*Herman.*

Lier, 1910.

F

# THE SEVENTH GRAVE

I OFTEN VISIT OUR CHURCHYARD. Especially in the evenings. When I walk through the flat fields that surround it far and wide, I always feel myself drawn to it.

I take a strange pleasure in wandering over the sods where the dead lie buried with a little plot of solemn flowers on their body and a crooked cross above their heads. It is as though I can feel the life of those dead people trembling and swelling beneath my feet, and can feel it creeping through my legs, feel it rising through my veins, scintillating through my whole body and warming my heart like new blood ... The pleasure of feeling the dead! ... Living in death while still alive! ... To feel one with them! ... To swim in the eternal mystery! ... The dead live in mystery, and their bodies alone chase the whispering of this mystery over people. My soul has an eternal thirst for mystery, for even when I travel through towns and villages, the churchyard is the very first place to which I turn my steps. It is always a joy to speak to the gravedigger, even if only about the weather and the skies.

I feel for each gravedigger something between admiration and fear, because does he not live on Death? He is a higher being than all of us, a man with a supernatural vocation, an intermediary between God and Death.

It is he who pulls us out of the world and executes God's fatal judgement: 'Ashes to ashes, dust to dust.' He could be a demi-god but his sly human nature prevents him. He does, however, stand at every funeral with a sad and severe face observing the pain of the good people, but inwardly he laughs and is glad, for each dead person pays him a toll as a farewell to this life. The more graves he has to dig the better. He wants nothing but dead people and if there are few fatalities he will pray to God to take people's lives . . . He becomes a demon, a vampire of souls!

Sometimes he can tell of dreadful things. And among the many stories I heard on my pilgrimages to unknown cemeteries one has stayed in my memory, apparently very ordinary and of little significance, but in reality one of the most shocking things one could ever think up. When it was told to me, I was staying for a few days on urgent business in a deserted little country town. It was the end of summer and nature was static and without life, as if it were musing on its death that was approaching.

On the very first day of my stay there, I had strolled to the churchyard after my day's work.

It lay lonely and abandoned in the scanty fields. It was a windy dusk, and deep in the west there was a dirty-yellow light, against which the churchyard stood out black and massive. The whole was an old Romanesque church, built in brown stone, which had fallen into ruin. Very high pillars bore crumbling arches, around which the sad ivy crept slowly upwards like the funerary song of medieval monks. The dark crowns of heavy poplars shivered above this silent ruin, and here and there dark cypresses stood motionless on the watery sods as if absorbed in sombre reflections on eternity and death.

Weeping willows drooped their disheartened branches

over black gravestones. And among them the many poor people's black crosses lay scattered in a disorderly fashion and displayed, as something useless and ridiculous in this great oblivion, the white names of those who lay crushed under the earth. Nothing broke this silent monotony with a joyful colour or sound. Everything was black and dark and dead. It was like the view of a town, which went on living in the past, raising itself in sombreness against the wide west like an awesome gripping hand, the hand of Death.

An anxious silence weighed on this motionless churchyard. Only now and then did a bunch of cawing crows swarmed from the mysterious depths of the ruin and spread out over the evening countryside like the doomed seed of the parable.

I wandered, restless and with a strange fear in my heart, among the silent pillars and blocks of stone. Suddenly it struck me how between the dark walls and pillars the house of the gravedigger came into view, white as a soul. The white shutters were already closed and on the first floor the white curtains were already drawn. Through the chinks in the shutters shone a red light. A pitiful bleating forced its way through the silence and filled my heart with dread . . .

I recovered from the fright and on looking round more closely, I noticed a black goat tied to a pillar by a hemp rope. It must be the gravedigger's goat, which chews the grass here, fed with the juices of the dead, in order to give him the white milk. It bleated pitifully in the evening, which was mysterious and descended anxiously over the world.

Now I was calm again and wanted to suppress that cowardly feeling of fear, I approached the house. But

I stopped, seeing with dismay a patch of corn, which, grey-gold in the evening, carried on an intimate dialogue with the white of the house.

Life in death! . . . What kind of strange gravedigger lived here, who broke his bread from the ashes of the dead and drank his milk from the juices flowing from their bodies? . . .

The following evening, I returned and saw the white house dimly beyond the ruins, and the black goat bleated and through the chinks in the shutters a flaming streak forced its way . . . And every evening I saw this, always the same, and it made me very afraid . . .

And the following Sunday, when I had no work, I went there in broad daylight and to my pained bewilderment found the shutters closed and the same pitiful red shaft of light trembling in the chinks.

I no longer knew what to think! . . .

Was the gravedigger himself perhaps lying there dead, without anyone knowing? I would have so liked to speak to him and hear from his mouth the mystery of this white house.

I returned at twilight, burning with a sickly longing to finally meet the gravedigger. I walked between the pillars and looking in all directions I saw a man in front of a small mound, motionless, staring at the late purple flowers blossoming at the foot of an iron cross. He was leaning on a long spade, in which the west shone like a flame at his feet. This must be the gravedigger. I went over to him, but he did not look up. He was an old man, small and thin, with a yellow face in which two small, deep-set eyes glinted. He was a real gravedigger, an earthworm, whom one would recognise as a gravedigger among thousands. I asked with a muffled voice whose grave this was.

He replied briefly and snappily, 'A dead person' and said no more. I felt that the man had no inclination to start up a conversation, but this white house with its eternal light in the chinks of the always closed shutters, that black goat, intrigued me so much that I wanted to know more, whatever the cost.

And I asked: 'What was his name, man?'

A tremor passed over his face, he closed his eyes as if he were in great pain and then opened them again and peered fixedly at the dark flowers. He was silent. And I went on: 'Are you frightened of Death and the dead?'

He straightened his back and asked me: 'Aren't you frightened of them?' And when I answered him with a convinced 'no', he laughed shrewdly and snapped at me: 'They all say that, because they have not yet seen the dormant power of Death in operation.'

I observed that Death only existed in and with the death of a human being . . .

But then, grabbing my hand, he looked at me sharply. He laughed bitterly, shook his head and said in muted tones, speaking very familiarly: 'That isn't true. Death is something apart . . . A Divinity that is around us, in us and everywhere! . . . Death fills everything! Everything lives on death. And when Death reveals itself in someone, he dies. It is like the fire that is hidden in the stone in a dormant condition and when it strikes another stone expresses itself as a spark. The fire was in the stone, if not it would not have been possible to get it out. And just as one must first strike the stone to awaken the spark, so must some reason or other evoke Death in our life. In that way we invoke Death ourselves. A look, a word, a simple gesture of the hand, a thought, unconscious confession of our life, can make Death rise up.

We don't know when we make that call, but we make it anyway . . . sometimes for ourselves . . . sometimes to awaken that sombre power in others! . . . for human souls criss-cross each other like the corridors of a great castle. There is a connection between all of us. Sometimes we become aware afterwards of our calling and can stop our death, prevent its operation, by invoking another power, stronger than Death . . . That power is sometimes as simple as it is great. But people don't know that! People don't know death . . .'

He suddenly fell silent. I remained looking at him in astonishment, dismayed by those strange, never before heard reflections. The man saw that. He sat down on a moss-covered stone and beckoned me to come and sit next to him. The branches of a weeping willow shed their tears on us in the evening light. I scarcely saw the crosses, fading dimly away in the darkness of the high arches. The white window, through which the light between the shutters streamed, appeared in the dark framing of two pillars. A cypress was silent just in front of us. And in the great heavy evening the man told a story in a dark voice. A brief gesture of the hand underlined his horrid words:

'It is already many, many years ago. And in spite of the fierce winter that had the land in its grasp, a terrible disease raged in these parts, consisting of cholera and plague. It dragged whole armies of lame, desperate people to the grave.

And here in our town the dreadful affliction swept away a third of the population with appalling speed, so that I had to dig holes from morning till evening with a stranger, in order to be able to keep up with the number of dead. So many died that on some days the dead did not find their graves open yet and had to wait under a freezing sky – we have no mortuary – and the families left without seeing their unfortunate kin buried. Then it was evening and night, as the graves became free, when by the light of a stable lantern we lowered the coffins into the earth. The terrible affliction lasted for many days and constantly worsened. People saw it as a punishment from God. A shudder of fear and despair went through the world. The thought of death struck everyone with dismay and broke the will of the boldest, making them helpless and cowardly. Everyone now turned to God, the only possible help that shone in their deep, dark misery. Those who had never prayed and had mocked everything that was at all religious, now crept in full view of everyone, with a rosary, over the chilly church stones and kissed with the utmost passion of hope and love the feet of a wooden Christ which had been worn away with kissing . . . People saw themselves standing there, naked and wretched before eternity and all their vanity lay crushed to dust . . . They would have done anything to escape Death. They gave away their gold, made penance, promised and fasted, boiled strange herbs and even resorted to magic . . . But particularly there was a tremendous flocking of desperate people to the St Rochus chapel, which over there in the fields, in the shadow of three magnificent poplars, was being gradually eaten away by the vagaries of time. The pilgrimage through the snow-covered fields was an awful sight.

Whole processions of hundreds of people went there daily. Priests in white vestments led them with the cross held aloft. They rang the booming alarm bell, spread clouds of incense and from their mouths pulled into a sombre expression came a weeping succession of entreating psalms.

And behind them, crowding close together, shivering with cold and fear, there followed thousands of people, loudly lamenting their suffering and terror and praying hopefully on large rosaries. Children, old men, women clutching infants flat to their cold breasts, young men, men, poor and rich, they all swarmed and huddled together, piled thickly, as if they wanted to hide in each other in order to escape Death. They were no longer people, but a long, lamenting mass of flesh, cringing before Death. The wild wind blew over them, whipping up fine sleet and dispersed their prayers and their monotonous song and threw them like insignificant, useless things across the lonely, white, endless plain. There remained only the sombre sound of the heavy bronze alarm bell, which like the lamenting throat of that great wretched mass, complained to deaf heaven. Their step was heavy and ponderous, and yet they moved fast to stand before the wooden statue, two fists in size, of St Rochus, which in pilgrim's dress, faded because of the capricious days of snow, frost, rain and sun, for years and years silent in his absent woodenness, with blue eyes that looked fixedly into eternity, one finger pointing to his wounded thigh, and with the other hand stroking a dog, which brought a roll, had stood abandoned and forgotten in the white latticed chapel, only occasionally greeted by a child or an old woman. And now everyone who could walk or be carried streamed and panted on their way to it.

And all those people sank down in front of it, full of love and confidence, and fell with outstretched begging arms into the slush and felt neither cold nor discomfort! Oh, when that dark mass lay there on the white ground, praying, weeping, with snow above and below them, surrounded by infinity and silence, it was as if the earth itself were praying to bring that wooden thing to life, which through a miraculous gesture must snuff out the ravaging affliction. But it stood there and looked motionless at the millions of snowflakes which swished wildly from a distance in horizontal flight.

And yet when returning those people's step was lighter; a new peace shone from their eyes, for the wooden statue – they knew not how – had given them hope. And on the careworn, bleak faces there was a suggestion of triumph over Death.

But the following day the graves opened again and new processions crowded past in the same wretched way.

It seemed as if human strength with all its thoughts and prayers no longer counted, and people were dead things and God and Heaven remained deaf as if they did not exist.

But the cruellest thing in those processions was the lamentation that poured from people's anxious mouths when they passed the churchyard. It was as if a searing, fearful burden fell on top of them.

A shiver of terror went through the whole procession, the one grabbed the other with clawing hands and the whole mass left the path and went across the fields. Fear flashed from their eyes, a muffled weeping rose above the sombre heads and their step quickened. A general sigh of relief was released from their fearful breasts, when they passed this place. It was as if they thought that here in the churchyard – where their dead lay and where they themselves might lie tomorrow –

Death resided in the flesh and from here exercised his power over the whole world.

Now, the plague was most dreadful. Searing pains forced their way through the belly, making people curl up, and a dark blue colour, under which the yellow of pus glimmered, covered the whole of the body. An hour after death the pus broke out of the body and dripped stinking from the open wounds. It was awful.

And I, poor soul, felt myself in that ravaging like something that stood apart. I helped Death, opened and closed graves, and in the evenings my exhausted callused hands hung from my tired arms. I felt as if I were standing outside the tide of fear.

It was as if my office immortalised me and assured me against Death. I had not the slightest fear of dying, I never thought of it, and when in the evening I saw my family praying in the red-gold glow of the flickering hearth fire, I looked down at it with indifference, like a child's game. It seemed to me that the wall of the churchyard cut us off from time, the world and Death!

But the day came that would cast me down from this proud life, outside the course of human affairs, back into the wretched existence of the sorely tried population. It was at that point that the sickness raged at its worst and people became almost crazy with great sadness and despair.

One morning I was ordered to dig graves for four Beguines, who had died of the infectious disease. I hastened to do this work, because that day it would of course not stop at those four graves, and many people would leave their dead bodies lying in the earth. When I finished the fourth grave at about midday, while the deal coffins were waiting, the tiny body of a four-month-old child was brought, and people came to ask me to dig a grave for an old man who had died that morning. There would certainly be more, according to what the bearers said, and the day before we had buried fourteen people. Now, on this day my assistant had not shown up for work, probably also infected by the disease. So, I did my very best to keep up with the dead they brought me, as the ground was hard and fine snow lashed me in the face like thin whips. The sixth grave was finished.

It surprised me that no more dead were announced. And then, to save time, I dug the seventh grave, for which there would soon be an occupant anyway. While I was doing this, the old man was brought, who with a short prayer by the priest was lowered into the grave before the eyes of the weeping family. Such was the end for all of them.

After their departure I hurried up and soon finished the seventh grave. I was about to start on an eighth one, but a pilgrimage to the St Rochus chapel was just going past. Everyone not hit by the scourge stumbled along in the foul weather and carried fear and wretchedness on their broken backs. I heard how their prayers choked as they approached this place and how a fearful mumbling rolled over their heads. I saw how they retreated from me into the fields, hastened their step and then continued on their weary way on the white path through the distant plain. The sound of the alarm bell boomed out through the quiet air. I thought how one of them shortly or tomorrow would be here under the ground, in the grave I had just dug. Then it struck my heart like a cold iron fist that I had made a grave not ordered for anyone! I went pale. Was this not a challenge to Death to fetch someone? . . .

I stared at the grave for a long time, which looked into my soul as if into an abyss. Would I not cause a person to die? I felt in truth that not one of our deeds is lost and that they have an effect on what we do not see. I wanted to fill in the grave at once, as if to prevent what may already have happened . . .

But when I was about to start I felt what I was doing was stupid! . . . I laughed at my naïve thoughts, threw the spade down into the hole to be sure not to do it and went home. Once that door had closed behind me I felt peace beating in my heart again!

I sat down by the hearth that flared up red and warmed my tingling hands and no longer thought of the grave. My wife and child did the housework silently, but soon they began to express their astonishment at the small number of people who had passed away today. Their words were full of happiness, since they saw the danger averted. It was as if they felt relieved of the fear and anxiety of the dreadful days. I peered through the window, through which I could see a part of the black mass of pillars and a large part of the wide fields. It remained unmarked by any human soul. The snow pricked against the window panes and the evening fell like impenetrable black rain over the wide world.

I went to shut the gate. No one moved there. The silence and the darkness were stretched over the earth as if eternally. As I came back I saw the grave that had put such fear into me just now. I laughed at it and felt happy that I had not given in to that impulse. When I got back inside the evening meal was steaming in the yellow lamplight. We ate in silence. Then we moved around the hearth to pray for our welfare and salvation. I occasionally looked at my wife and child and felt happy, while outside wretchedness reigned, to be here so cosily together.

The comforting glow of the many-flamed hearth which lit up their faces was like the visible prayer that they prayed with eyes closed to the bone rosary . . . Then we went to bed. Our child, a girl of thirteen, slept next to our room, and since she had grown up there was no light in our bedroom.

When I was lying in bed next to my wife and was gradually getting warm, I was filled with an unusually beneficent calm. I was so happy. My soul was as if drunk with pleasure. I soon fell asleep, but sleep, which closed my eyes to the world, brought me a frightening dream: I saw the ground of the churchyard rise up and shift slowly past me. Suddenly it stopped and right ahead of me I saw dark against its whiteness the seven graves I had dug today. I saw the graves open and saw through the coffins. There lay next to each other the four Beguines in black with their hands folded, next to them the baby curled up, and the old man with one eye open and stretched as stiff as a plank. The seventh grave was empty and dark. But when I looked more closely I saw something become visible, which gradually became clearer. It was a human figure, it was a man; but then I suddenly saw to my great dismay that it was none other than myself, lying there dead. I started awake, gasped for breath and wanted to scream out my fear. But I felt the darkness hanging around me and my nightshirt sticking sweatily to my body. I let out a sigh of relief and was glad that it was only a dream. But then suddenly my earlier premonition about this seventh grave flashed back and told me I was the one who must die.

I felt the hairs on my head standing on end. Had I

not dreamt it? Didn't God himself send me a sign? ... And now the regret welled up in me forcefully that I had not filled and closed up the grave and had dismissed my premonition so foolishly as a low impulse. That dream now convinced me that I was soon to die. I knew it irrevocably, just as I know that a star, scarcely born in the sky, already extinguished, still sends us its light even after years and years, while it no longer exists. The icy cold breath of death went through my bones. I would not survive the night. And instantly I felt in pure imagination the crushing pain of cholera pushing through my body, I saw myself already dying and gasping out my life, and I felt myself falling into a bottomless, ghastly darkness, always eternally falling, towards a sharp glowing pin to which I never came closer, though that did not relieve me of the terror of landing on it. I also heard the earth, shaken out by a strange hand, thudding onto my coffin ... I grew dizzy at the clear thought of death, and I had to stifle a piercing scream in my throat for fear of my wife ... I did not want to die, I would fill that grave first thing and so save my life. I intended already to get up ... but I heard my wife's breath going up and down. This paralysed me. I knew that she woke up at the slightest noise and then I would have to confess everything to her; she would laugh at me and consider me a fool. And that stopped me. So I lay there full of despair, awaiting my death. It was as if I were going to burst. I wept. I began to pray, to pray as if I wanted to fill the grave with prayers, although I knew that in this case prayer was no good. I gnashed my teeth with rage. In order to save myself I must fill the grave with the earth I had taken out. I shivered so much that the bed jolted, my throat became dry and tightened. I could no longer stand it, it was as if I were on fire. I rose silently from bed, looked for water, which I swallowed greedily. The cold struck my sweaty body, increasing the gooseflesh on my skin. There I stood then, I who must directly die in order to be buried in the grave dug by myself.

I approached the window through which I saw looming up in the dark far above my head the proud pillars and walls. It was no longer snowing. My eyes searched for the grave that I could not find, as it was too dark. I widened my eyes in the pitch-black night and looked . . . Suddenly a silver light shone from heaven, which with a full beam lit up the snow-covered churchyard in the night.

The black ruin was now like a silent curse, standing out dark against the whiteness. I no longer knew what was happening, was afraid and expected to see something massive and horrible, but the light remained there motionless as a house. Only then did I realise that it was the moon, which had broken through the clouds behind our house. And in the moonlight I saw between the crosses and the dark ruin the open grave, black as a blot of ink. There I would lie tomorrow, I who had dug it and was now looking at it! God! I have never felt such terror! Was there nothing then that could save me! . . . And was I to let myself be dragged from the world like a lamb! Did I not have any will left! . . . And was not the grave itself my salvation? . . . Why should I pray when the remedy was there for the taking? . . . And my wife and child had heard nothing!

They slept soundly. I wanted to take advantage of the opportunity.

The intention brought a smile to my lips. I got dressed carefully and stole softly to the door. The latch gave a short, dry squeak. I stopped still, my wife shifted in bed, and not feeling me next to her she asked, "Where are you?" My hair stood on end, as if I had committed the greatest evil in the world, and I answered hesitantly that I wanted to drink some salt water, since the evening meal was keeping me awake. I heard her sink back into the pillows with a contented "Oh". Then I charged downstairs – happy as someone carrying heaven in his arms – to nip my fate in the bud. Trembling, I opened the front door. At the same time, it was as if an invisible naked being sprang around my body and pressed me desperately to her limbs.

My throat was squeezed shut and I had to gasp for breath. I dismissed this feeling. But I was startled when I saw how low close to the earth dark clouds reared up, like huge boulders, here and there lit by the moon, which must be behind our house.

I did not dare go any further; but I had to go on to prevent my death! When I moved out of the shadow of the house, my shadow suddenly shot forward like a snake, rustled across the snow between the houses and remained looking at me as the sudden apparition of a demon on a moonlit pillar. It was quiet. It seemed as if all the world were gripped in an iron silence. Nothing moved but the heavy beat of my fearful heart. For I was truly afraid in the nocturnal moonlit silence, among all the dead, to be the only living point. Something stroked my face like the gentle caressing of cold hands. Were those the souls of the dead, which were rising up and wanted to kill me? Was I supposed to be afraid, I who had buried them myself? . . . My heart shrank, my legs wobbled under my heavily breathing body and it seemed to me as if life were breathed into the crosses and they were opening and closing their arms like dumb people crying for help. And that silence, that silence! I thought I was dying and wanted to cry for help, for now my premonition was proving true. But my life! The terror of dying made the courage flare up in me. Yonder lay the open grave, like a black wound in white flesh. The certainty that I would be saved by filling it stiffened my will and my strength. And I started running, jumped over the crosses, stumbled, got up again, hurried on and found myself in front of the grave. I wanted to set straight to work but could not find the spade. I remembered having thrown it into the grave! So I must go into the hole to get it out! And this struck me with new terror and paralysed my will. I would never get out again. There I stood again like a child lost in a wood, who does not dare take a step, believing it will be attacked by a wild animal.

Everything was working against me! It was as if God himself wanted the grave to be filled only with my body. I became desperate and stood there in front of the grave digging into my hair with my hands. Suddenly, as if I had been pushed, I leapt into the dark grave. If I had to go in anyway, it could happen just as well now as later! I picked up the spade from under the snow and clambered out again and laughed at the fact that my premonition deceived me so badly. And I thought: what if the premonition to fill the grave were also misleading me? . . . It was already so late and I was still alive, I had even trodden on the bottom of the grave and still hadn't died? Wasn't it perhaps the darkness that had frightened me? . . . And I was again hesitant and full of inner torment. I swore and wept with impatience. What was I to do?

Fear had its hooks in me and foolishness mocked

in my ear! I didn't dare do anything. And how could I know *what* to do? . . .

Wouldn't God himself give me a sign? But the night remained wonderfully still and the moon cast noiselessly, from between two steep cliffs of clouds, its green light over the snow-covered earth. I felt that I was not allowed to, and could not, decide alone. God must intervene. I looked for something that would give me a sign! Suddenly a thought came to me that I found ridiculous, that reminded me of the superstition of children, but which I immediately carried out. I reached for a coin in my pocket. If I should bring it out with heads on top, I must fill the grave; if it was tails I could leave without worries. Yes, I, human being and gravedigger, was descending to a ridiculous means of finding out the truth! It was like a rune through which God was to speak . . . Full of fear I took out the coin and turned it towards the moonlight; it was heads. Great perturbation took hold of me. And without even thinking that it might be chance, I hastily grabbed the spade, planted it in the pile of dirt, and shovelled the clumps of earth liberally into the grave. This patting and banging in a grave containing no one, and at night too, made a much more powerful impression than filling an ordinary grave. I went on working and laughed, because I was to be spared! I knew very well that tomorrow I would blush at this, but nothing would have happened! When I had filled a few spadesful, I suddenly heard a muffled voice, as if coming out of the ground, call my name three times. I leapt back in alarm, dropped the spade and stood there as if turned to stone . . . I could not move a step, as if the marrow of my bones had turned to lead. I dare not look round, fearing to see a dead person behind me who had called me . . . The sweat poured off my face and slowly, carefully and fearfully I turned my head. A light was shining yonder. It was the window of my bedroom, at which a light had been lit.

I immediately realised that my wife, worried by my long absence, had called me and lit a candle. But now I had to go and leave the grave open. I wept with despair! The further I went from the grave, the closer I came to death. I thought I would burst with hopelessness and felt all too keenly that God wanted me to be buried tomorrow . . . My wife must know nothing at all! I walked hurriedly, carefully opened the door, went into the kitchen and pumped hard to make her believe that I had really gone downstairs for the reason I told her. Then I went upstairs. And again, my wife called out my name, trembling and fearful. I became afraid; something must have happened! I hastened my step and opened the door of the room, which was filled with candlelight. It amazed me greatly to see my wife sitting on the bed, with our child clutched in her arms.

A smile glistened on her lips when she saw me and the fear disappeared from her eyes. But then hastily, with her eyes still open wide, her voice whispered to me anxiously: "Where did you get to? . . . Did you see him? Did you hear him . . . Oh, you were gone so long, I called you and you didn't answer, then I got up and went, I don't know why, – it was like an inspiration from God – to look out of the window and – O Lord – I saw a black man in the churchyard who was digging a grave; it was the devil, the devil . . . digging a grave for us."

Her words ran like a splash of boiling pitch through my brain. I saw her with that rigid fear of death, which must have been in my countenance too. The confession, for I wanted to tell her everything, to raise her from that dreadful condition, was already on my lips, but again I saw the ridiculousness of my thoughts looking mockingly at me, and I said that there couldn't have been anyone in the churchyard, that the gate was closed, that she had seen the shadow of a cross or stone and everything that could put her mind at rest, but she stuck to her story and she wanted to pray for God to destroy the devil's power.

I discovered my own situation underlying her words and the three of us prayed on our knees by the bed, in the motionless light of the white, slender candle. And I cried, cried silently at the result of my deed, which could not be long in coming. We went to bed, my wife wanted to leave the candle burning and she clamped her arms around my body and feeling safer, she soon fell into a deep, heavy sleep. Our child was back in the other room and was probably so shaken by mother's words that she lay with her head under the blankets, since I could no longer hear her breathing . . . I wanted to stay awake, awaiting great Death and praying the whole time for my salvation. But I don't know what it was that made me so tired.

The candlelight caressed my eyes, the pleasure of seeing light did me good like a bath of warm water. And without myself knowing how, I must have slowly fallen asleep, fast asleep . . . For I was not a little surprised in the morning that I woke from sleep and was still in the same room and hence not dead. At first it seemed to me that I was in another world, but when I felt my wife next to me, saw the white curtains and the silent objects, I understood everything and the truth rushed through my being like a waterfall. So, the premonition, the fear had been imagination! A great joy pounded through my heart. I was still alive! I had not given in to my weak imagination! So this grave was nothing but an ordinary pit! A great feeling of contentment descended upon me, and I remained still, not thinking of anything, happy at my victory. Next to me my wife was asleep and her breath went calmly up and down like a distant song of the sea. I listened involuntarily for the breathing of my child. I could not hear anything. In the room everything remained deathly still. A strange fear again came over me. I became anxious and everything turned and danced before my eyes! I jumped out of bed and went to the room. But I recoiled in terror, uttered a raw cry and had to grab the wall so as not to stumble. In the white bed, half-naked, curled up, lay my child, dark blue as a slate, with wide unfocused eyes, in which nothing but the whites could be seen, and a wide-open mouth, from which a thick blue tongue bulged. She was dead! Died of the pestilence! . . . I howled like a beast, cursed and damned the whole world.

I danced with rage, for everything flickered brightly in my mind: the open grave, which I had made for her! I was my child's murderer! . . . My wife came rushing up. Oh, when she saw this most dreadful sight, she stared straight ahead wild-eyed, a lump blocked her bare throat and she collapsed like a rag on the blue corpse, under which the pus was already glimmering!

The sickness could not have lasted long and the child had not even been able to cry out, for her tongue was so swollen that it must have stifled all sound.

Suddenly my wife raised herself upright and cried cuttingly at me: "You see now! Didn't I tell you it was the devil who was digging the grave for her! . . ."

Now I had to speak, I was already opening my mouth, but she screamed loudly, reproachfully in my face: "Are you saying I'm lying? . . . that I'm lying? . . . Come with me then, come!" Before I could make a move to stop her she rushed downstairs in her nightgown. I ran after her, but she charged outside in the icy winter air and ran as fast as she could to the place where the grave was, where she stopped and shouted to me: "Look here, look here at how I'm lying . . . Here he stood, here he stood and here is a grave." Then I grabbed her, carried her back inside and weeping and sobbing made my confession. I told her everything. But she did not listen, appeared not to understand me and remained staring motionless ahead of her with great fear in her eyes and whispered to herself, withdrawing into herself: "See, there is the devil, there behind that cupboard, see him laugh, see him holding our child in his black arms! . . ." Then it seemed to me as if everything broke! My wife was mad! . . .

My child was the last victim of the terrible disease. And my child was buried in the grave I myself had dug, There in front of you, this grave with the dark mauve flowers. This is it. And there in that white house, in the lamplight, my wife sits, lame and mad, still seeing the devil before her. The shutters and blinds are forever closed because if she sees the churchyard she starts raging. That's how it is now after so many years! And still I am convinced' – at this point the man got up – 'that if I had not dug this grave or had filled it completely, that fatal event would not have happened! Judge for yourself . . .'

And the man went away in silence towards his white

house . . . A long, solemn silence fell. The yellow light from the west was extinguished. An owl whooshed past mysterious and dark, so that the wind from its wings brushed my face. I heard the sickly bleating of the goat, loud in the wide evening, and then I went away, as if I had felt Death.

F

# THE WHITE VASE

THE WORLD LAY ON MY HEART like a heavy weight, and I was forced to abandon human company in order to give expression to the workings of my soul in some silent place. The time had come when it was languishing, exhausted and stifled amid all the rottenness of society, and yearned to enjoy a wholesome life of its own. I left for an extended stay in a Trappist monastery, which I knew was located in the wide, flat, arid heathlands, with open horizons all around like the sea.

I had been there a few days; but how those had actually rolled by in the well of time I could no longer say. The brightness of the third day too was fading into darkness without my having undertaken any action, when as the sun set I realised I was a completely changed man, and that a strange mood had arisen in me so simply, so imperceptibly, that it seemed as if I had always been like this.

Had these two days of prayer and silence freed my soul of its worldly burden, so that it only now made itself felt?

A strange, nameless feeling had arisen in me, a kind of unconscious terror of something far away, whose tangible presence I nevertheless felt in myself and all around me. I tried to push it away, but I was fooling myself, because the thing was lodged in my body like the blood in my heart, and it began to spread, like the mist that rises from the meadows at evening. I became afraid of what surrounded me. I suddenly felt the dreariness of the country in which I stood so utterly lost and alone. The bare sandy heath, dotted only sparsely with wild cypress trees, stretched endlessly into the distance, far, far away until it stood out dark and sharp as gorse against the pale sky. Neither woods nor towers awakened any hope of continuing human habitation; it was as if the world ended right there and I myself became the boundary of human life. And very low overhead were thick, heavy banks of dark-blue clouds. Only when the resonant bell of the monastery had stopped ringing did I notice its sound, and as it hung silently in its distant tower, a sudden arresting silence descended on the countryside. This caught my attention, and I strained to hear that silence, and I heard nothing, nothing, nothing at all, an unimaginable silence. Because I was feeling so anxious, I began searching for sound. At first in the distance, for the barking of a dog, the rumble of a train, but nothing came from afar, there too things were in the thrall of that strange motionlessness of sound, and the cypress trees were stuck there like iron skittles, the dry, prickly wands of gorse thrust from the ground as if petrified; if one had moved around me, I would have heard, so motionless was the silence and no wind, not a breath came, and I waited; but nothing came, everything was held down by that great power, hitherto unknown to me.

And my own heart stood still. I wanted to break the silence with a cry, a scream, but it was choked in my throat, like a soap bubble bursting.

Was that eternal motionlessness preparing to explode at any moment in a thousand-fold boom of thunder?

Oh, it weighed on my soul like a stone, that unending plain. It made me close my eyes and I became so afraid that I started and hurried away to the monastery . . .

Only as I stood beneath the monastery gates did I dare look round, and there, right ahead of me, in the centre of the gloomy avenue of poplars, very low on the horizon, was a half moon, ungainly and blood-red.

When I arrived in the cold church, the monks in their richly draped white habits were praying in silence, and one brother was just lighting a long candle, which dotted half the mysterious darkness with a fiery flower, and the eternal sanctuary lamp, floating in red glass, brushed a very thin stripe of pink onto the Gothic vaults. Three monks in brown habits each grasped a bell rope and began pulling; booming sounds rang out above my head from the tower and soared away across the mysterious evening countryside. The church throbbed with them. And now the monks started praying aloud in Latin.

The prayers were chanted. Rapid words were mumbled, at times sustained for longer, at times abrupt, but always equally dry, without surges or swells, and it went on and on, and as it grew it became repugnant, and increased like something that would never stop and would continue forever. It was as though a single person were praying; eventually one forgot the monks and it was nothing but an accumulation of hollow words in the useless dark. It was as if these eighty monks were one creature with one soul and one thought, with one heart and one will; like a machine with various cogs operated by a leaden hand. It troubled my heart, and I thought of the night before me. My room was down an endless white corridor of the deserted wing of the monastery, where I had to spend the night completely alone. I was terrified of something that I felt intensely, but could not define. I had the impulse to go home at once. But I was unsure of the way and the nearest station was over an hour from the monastery. I was about to stifle my terror with prayer, when the praying suddenly stopped and an oppressive silence ensued, which fortunately did not last long.

The monks were now standing facing the altar with their arms opened wide and stretched out towards the image of the Virgin Mary, Greek in its loveliness, that stood above the altar in the feeble glow of the candles like an approaching vision of a holy twilight. Suddenly the stops of the organ opened and gave forth sweet, calm tones, which gently filled the church one by one, creating a limpid song that made me forget my fear. And with a clear, warm voice the cantor sang: *Salve*. It was heavy with profound tenderness and deep faith, and the other monks immediately responded in unison with *Regina* and sang the sacrosanct words of the old hymn. The air trembled with sublime love and divine purpose, with a deeply-hidden undertone of extreme suffering. The song swelled and bent, surging to and fro like the song of the sea. It was as though from time to time a wind caught the sounds, carried them up to heaven, and descended again when the time was ripe. And it mounted in ecstasy like the flames of a fire, and the organ mingled and wreathed and sprinkled its full-grown clear notes among them, extending the song higher and firmer in its beauty. It was like a host of white flowers, blossoming one by one around the mysterious silence where God himself dwelt.

I had forgotten my trouble; tears trickled down my cheeks and I expected, with the simplicity of a child, that the white image of the Virgin, affected by all that profound devotion, would move as a sign that our prayers had been heard.

Suddenly a silence descended on the church, the monks were absorbed in inward prayer. The time was approaching when I would have to go to my room; my heart stood still at the prospect. And the monks shuffled mysteriously down the long corridors, the tiny candle was snuffed out, the doors closed and the church was left in cold silent darkness, in which the blood-red sanctuary lamp with its eternal glow flickered like an eye opening and shutting.

Without kneeling I left the dais and stood in the long white corridor. I stood there; in the far distance, lit by a reddish candle flame, was a large, ugly statue of the Virgin Mary. Then I crept down the corridor to my room, which I plunged wildly into. I bolted the door, lit the candle, and slumped into a chair, feeling half relieved of the great burden weighing on my heart. I was about to breathe a sigh of relief, but when I saw the white candlelight falling on my pale and bony hands, I became alarmed and again such a great silence descended, but now it was as though it were tangible, cloaking and enclosing everything. It was as if the whole room were brim-fulf of water that was forcing me into the chair and my arms down onto its arms. I tried to laugh at my fear and foolishness, but I couldn't because I could feel that there was something too serious behind it. After all I was completely alone in that wide wing of the monastery where the holy relics were stored, filled with bones, skeletons and skulls. Yet it was not those dead things that I was afraid of; my heart was seized by such a sense of doom, which may always be present, but which can only manifest itself in silence and solitude. I did not dare follow my thoughts to their logical conclusion, but they kept recurring, gaining in clarity: I would die here tonight . . . I would have liked to go outside, sleep on the bare, frightening heath, but I was sitting here as in a secure prison, the warders of which lay dead. I was so convinced of my powerlessness in the face of what was imminent, that I abandoned all hope and no longer believed I would live to see morning. I no longer dared move; I felt cold and bathed in sweat all over my body. I thought neither of home nor of my parents or other things that I had left behind forever, it was as if they had never existed and I had been sitting here like this forever; I had eyes only for the things around me. Next to me on the table, which was covered in a white cloth, was a porcelain vase with two lilies in it. It caught my attention because I suddenly noticed its beauty. I admired its gently swelling shape. It was so pure and elegant and was undecorated. It was nothing but a curving line upwards from base to the top, where it opened into a smooth straight neck.

The candlelight played beautifully around it, splashing luxuriantly down on it in the centre, fading almost into invisibility on either side. Right in the middle the light continued to penetrate, caressed the hidden stem of the lily and brushed the back of the vase, where it cast a luminous shadow, a white shadow on the table. I wanted to possess that vase. And that calm beauty, which kept to a single line, made me forget my horrid thoughts. Then I noticed that everything in my room was white: the wall, the closed curtains of my bed, the vase, the table. All that whiteness seemed to wrap my warm heart in snow and I looked for something dark.

My eyes moved towards the window; there were white curtains over this too, but one had been drawn and revealed a coal-black window pane. I sprang to my feet in amazement: there at the window was an ugly, pale man's head with a wild beard and huge eyes, which gave off a deathly yellow gleam. I was about to scream, when I saw that my anxious face was reflected in the pane. Now I could no longer control it, everything was conspiring to make me more afraid, even my own image. I blew out the light, and too cowardly to get undressed, jumped into bed with ruff collar, stockings and all, and hid under the sheets.

And now I felt satisfied and without fear, as if all that unpleasantness were entering me from outside and was being excluded by the cover, but again that did not last long; I was gasping for breath and lifted the covers a fraction, I felt the cool air approaching while I listened. There was a deep silence in my room, but in the corridor I could hear the heavy ticking of the large clock I knew was there. That was something new that now grabbed my attention, I followed along with the sound of the ticking; I was greatly startled when I heard that this noise was growing louder and louder until it was no longer ticking, but the steps of someone slowly coming closer; I heard it clearly. The person came to my door; then the sound stopped and began again, but returned the way it had come; it slowly retreated until in the distance it again assumed the sound of the ticking of the clock on whose face death was swinging a scythe.

I soon set out to discover what these steps actually were, since I was not dreaming; I pinched my cheeks very hard; no I wasn't dreaming; were the steps perhaps those of a monk, coming to listen to see if I were asleep?

It couldn't be anyone else, as there was no one in that wing of the monastery. I was about to reassure myself with that thought, when again I heard the usual tick-tock gradually changing into the same step, again, like before, coming slowly closer. I listened, sitting upright in my bed; my beard was wet with sweat and the hair on my head stood on end. And the step came closer, closer, stopped still again in front of my door and then turned back, very slowly, and again merged into the ticking of the clock. Now I no longer knew what to think. It was definitely not a human being, since the sound of the steps, rising and then merging back into the ticking of the clock, was far too strange for that. So what was it . . . ? The power of death that was to come for me in person tonight? . . . The power of death that as it walked down the white corridor was waiting for the exact time to throttle me? My heart pounded like the banging of a child's frightened fist on a dark door. I listened, but only ticking reached my ears. I suddenly became convinced that the steps, returning a third time, would finish their work. I shuddered. I now felt the finality of what I had thought; I knew I was so helpless, so insignificant in the face of that great power. I would have to die here, very soon, so far from home, in the night, in a monastery full of silent monks! The other facts about which my presentiment had always proved true surged up and strengthened my perceptions. I listened, things were the same in the corridor and suddenly a lucid thought went through my brain: I might just have time before the steps returned to creep into the adjacent room and so deceive the *thing* that was about to return; *it*, not finding me here, might stop looking further. This resolution gave me very little hope, but made me laugh, since something that is bound to happen to you will happen in any case, with no regard for ocean depths or heavenly heights. On the other hand I knew that we can sometimes turn around a predetermined life with a simple gesture. I got up, picked up my slippers and opened the door very, very softly, and I went from my dark room into the lonely corridor and closed the door again extremely carefully. Then I looked down the corridor, which was as lugubrious and mysterious as it had been just now. The mysteriousness, which was identified with the corridor, seemed to have become tangible. And the candle in front of the statue of Our Lady lit it and the clock gave it a sound; yet there was no sign of that other *thing*, still that *something* could be heard, but not seen – perhaps it was standing there before me, peering at the end of my life with great gleaming cat's eyes. I felt unsteady on my feet in my dismay, but suddenly plucked up my courage and went to the other room, bolted the door and pushed the first chair I could find in front of it. I looked for the bed and again hid beneath the sheets, but now curled up, hands clasped over my ears and praying. But I did not illumine the words of the prayers either with my feelings or thoughts. I did nothing but think, think of the thing that was approaching and that I had tried to fool, and filled with intense fear I awaited the outcome. The thoughts stampeded through my head like maddened goats in the night; I shivered and the sweat ran from my head and arms, it trickled and sometimes tickled, but I did not wipe it off, I no longer dared move: only now and then, when it became stiflingly hot, did I raise the bedclothes a little with my elbow for fresh air. It continued, on and on as if two days of light and dark were passing over me. I dared not take my hands from my ears; I did not want to hear a thing, anything. And so I lay there waiting in the dreadful uncertainty whether death would find me or not. And I lay there even longer cringing with terror, until I suddenly turned my head to the side and raised a corner of the bedclothes. I don't know how, but suddenly my blood, which seemed to have solidified in my veins, began to flow and effervesce like the sea. I had seen a patch of faint grey daylight. The scant light, scarcely visible, drove out my fear, and I jumped out of bed full of happiness like someone raised from the dead. Look! the first glow of day was appearing beyond the world. I laughed with joy and began to think it was just the darkness that had provoked all those dismal thoughts.

The bell in the tower struck two-thirty. So everyone was still sleeping their monks' sleep. So I would have to wait before I could go outside. I was about to sit on a chair when I became curious and wanted to see the abandoned room. God knows what had happened there. My God, the door of the room was wide open! . . . I went closer, and a violent gust of air struck me in the face; look, the window was wide open too! I went in, God! on the white sanded planks the beautiful vase lay smashed to smithereens, while the grey daylight crept over it. The stately lilies seemed to be buried under it, with their calyxes crumpled and bruised. Only the base of the beautiful vase remained in the centre of the table.

For all my deep astonishment I felt inundated with happiness; that open door, that open window and that broken vase! Oh, my God! I knew exactly what had happened! My presentiment had been correct! And suddenly the bells rang out in all their bronze richness! From far away shuffling and scuffing approached; the monks had got up, and I waited for the kitchen monk of the closed order to come and prepare my breakfast in the kitchen. When I heard him turn the key in the lock of the gate, I rushed downstairs to tell him what had happened. He was astonished to see me so early, but I explained everything, my premonition, my terror, the changing of rooms and the dreadful discovery of the beautiful white vase. The dear man was completely carried away by my story, and when I had finished he said, shaking his head and with his eyes closed, with great conviction: 'It was the devil.'

I knew differently and the very same day I returned home, for how would I dare spend the next night there? As I walked across the broad heath in the morning sunshine, I rejoiced at the top of my voice, for I had evaded death! . . . I had fooled death!

# THE UNKNOWN

He, Hendrik by name, stood waiting for the girl named Begga on the stone bridge, under which passed the grey waters of the Nete, which wound its way from one horizon to the other through autumn fields now covered by evening. There was a shiver of sharp cold and the land lay dark and wide as a bottomless pit. Here and there a puddle of rainwater shone dull-white like an eye. The sky was piled with black, motionless clouds, which were like extinguished coals, and through the disorderly cracks and holes the dirty yellow of the sunset leaked.

Just as that sky weighed on the earth, so life lay shattered on his heart.

He would have liked to tear his chest open to give his heart more room to beat, to toll like a bell. But it hung like a lump of zinc in his chest. It had always been like this and he knew that it would stay like it. A curse hung over him. Therefore, he had called on Death, who was the only one who could roll the heavy stone from his heart.

And she too, whom he was waiting for and was called Begga, was crushed by life and hence had fallen in love with Death.

Begga and Hendrik loved each other so! They were born for each other. They were both young and they had wanted to embark upon life together, like thousands of others. But her parents had rebelled and resisted expressly the notion that their only child should marry a sick young man, and his sisters, who already had grey hair and were unmarried, wanted to keep their dear brother with them. They would rather throw all their money in the water than see it fall into the hands of the daughter of the woman who had first made them out to be as ugly as sin. Hendrik had soon fallen into a dispute with his sisters, had left them, and now lived alone in a little house and earned some money by drawing lace patterns.

Then there had come the great sorrow for him and Begga. They sought each other in secret, but everywhere the sisters or the mother tracked them down. He was so broken by this that he neglected his work. And he ate his last cents. He suffered greatly and was deathly sad. They could not go on living like this, they both knew that only too well, and the bond between them was too strong to separate. And then the idea gradually emerged of dying together. They would do it in that water, which moved so silently and mysteriously through the evening. He saw the water that was like floating, cold lead. And he loved it, because it seemed so heavy and was so silent. Because it would cover them forever in its dark depths, because they would lie in it together and feel no more of that heavy pressure of life but would enjoy an eternal unconscious rest and peace. He did not think about the water possibly being cold, he thought only of the happiness that awaited them in the depths. And in that resided precisely the goodness of Death . . . He felt for the rope, which was to tie them together, since they wanted their bodies to be bound together in death.

Here they would drop from the bridge, there would be only a great splashing and rocking of water and it would close over them forever.

He peered through the darkness to see whether she was approaching yet. There was no one. The land lay silent and black, the dirty yellow behind the rocky clouds had gone out. Now there was only the darkness and him. And he suddenly felt as if there were no one alive on earth except him. He became afraid in this silent, dark space, so great and so wide. He had wanted her to be with him, very quickly, for he was afraid without her. That was how it always was; when she was not with him, he felt he lacked something, knew there was a gap in his heart and was full of unrest.

Was she not coming? Had she been frightened by Death? . . . He knew her view that Death is a gate, which leads to the conscious life of the soul, and that she wanted to die in this water in order to live on forever with his soul. She thought Death was the most certain way of always being with him and always enjoying his love.

He heard dull steps climbing out of the darkness. He listened. It came closer and then he heard a rustling of skirts. It was Begga. He immediately clutched her tender body to his, pressed a kiss on her forehead, which was tucked away under a black shawl. He then let go of her again, and they stood there silently unable to say a word.

'Do you have the rope with you?' she asked suddenly.

'Here it is . . .' She immediately fell about his neck and wept. They both wept.

'Come,' he said, 'there's nothing else for it.'

'Oh God, how happy I shall be . . . Hendrik,' the words of gratitude welled from her mouth.

'What did your mother say when you left?'

'She doesn't know.'

'Where did you get to for so long?'

'Where?' she asked stuttering. 'In church . . . I went to pray that God may forgive us, and that we may be happy.' A silence ensued. They went to the stone edge of the bridge and peered through the darkness.

'It's cold,' he said, and he added with difficulty: 'Is it dark enough yet, do you think?'

'Is there anyone about?' she asked. They looked around, but the darkness hung everywhere like a thick curtain.

'There's no one,' he said. He took her hand in his and they were silent. They were silent in spite of themselves, for their hearts were weighed down with unspoken words, which they could not get out. He took her in his arms, as if to make her feel what he could not say, and she put her head on his neck.

'Are you doing it with love?' he asked, just to break the silence.

'Do you dare doubt?' she asked gravely.

'No . . . no, but it is such a great moment . . .'

'Are you afraid, perhaps?' she said then.

'You know very well, Begga,' he answered forcefully.

'Yes, I know,' she said happily and pulled him to her.

'Do you think it's time yet?'

'Yes, it's dark and no one's there.' He uncoiled the rope. Then she said: 'Wasn't it a good idea to drown ourselves bound together? . . . Otherwise one of us might perhaps try to save themselves, since they say that water is terrifying.'

'If it were me, oh I would not leave you alone, Begga,' he said with conviction. 'When I think how we came together, what we have been through and suffered, then I feel we cannot be separated, that is why no rope is necessary here. There is an unbreakable rope joining you and me, which we cannot shake off. Do you know what I sometimes think? . . . That we have only one heart.'

'I sometimes think that too,' she said. 'There is something in us that draws us together . . . I feel this better than I can say it. And I think, Hendrik, that if I had to lie alone in this water, that I would rise up and get you. Oh, because I love you so much.'

'And I too,' he sobbed . . . And they wept.

'We shouldn't have met each other,' she said.

He said: 'It is as if we already knew each other when we came out of God's hands. We had to know each other.'

'We must die together too. We shall be so happy there. Let's do it now,' she sobbed.

'Yes,' he decided.

It was as if the darkness turned to stone, it was so dark, but yonder on the edge of the horizon, toward which the water wound its way, there suddenly glowed between the cracks and splits in the clouds the blood of the rising moon. It trembled and lived on the water.

There were no sounds. But suddenly there was a heavy, muffled step on the dyke. They looked round in alarm, fearing that it was the mother or the sisters. He quickly put the rope away and she pulled the shawl further over her head. They did not move. The steps sounded closer and came on to the bridge; they were heavy hobnailed boots, which rang on the tops of the bumpy cobbles of the bridge. It was a fisherman, who with a gruff 'good evening' went on and descended the dyke next to the bridge, where a rowing boat was moored. With a jump he was on it and then began fiddling about with poles and clinking iron hooks. It was the eel-catcher from the night before last, who stayed here fishing for a whole night.

They were now very sorry not to have jumped into the water already. They did not dare speak. But he tugged her by the sleeve and they walked onto the dyke, past the fishing boat, towards the horizon.

When they were far enough away and the fisherman could no longer hear them, she said: 'It's a shame.'

'He's going to stop there anyway,' he whispered. 'Let us go on, yonder by the second bend.' And they went there quickly in silence. The pitch-black night, into which the moon's blood dripped, was frightening and horrid to see.

When they got there, they looked round; the fisherman was hidden far away over there beyond the reeds. So they could easily receive Death here. But she, Begga, was very cautious and asked: 'Let's go a bit further.'

They went on. She was very tired and trembled as she held his arm. Now the clouds broke open again and it was as if the sky was aflame again on that side. The matte brightness moved dully into the darkness. Then they saw in the weary light how on the narrow dyke a hollowed-out, age-old willow trunk leaned over the silent water. 'Here's a good place,' she said.

And Hendrik, showing her the rope, said: 'Shall I tie it round us?' And he bound the rope twice round their limbs, which were pressed together in such a way that he could with difficulty tie the two ends together in a knot. The glow of the moon lay across their faces, which were pale with mad eyes. They looked at each other. And then suddenly something welled up in their hearts and they both burst into sobbing and weeping. They said nothing more. Their arms wrapped round their bodies and they pressed their heads together. The tears of both mingled. The willow trunk beside them stood there like a human being. They shuffled their feet forward to the low, smooth dyke . . .

Another step, and another, and they lost their footing. She uttered a sharp shriek. They loosened their arms in waving, the rope came undone and they fell separately with a dull splash into the water. The water closed over them and drove great splashing waves irregularly across the wobbling surface, so that the sparse reeds bent and sighed.

Then it was still again as if nothing had happened, and through a great crack in the clouds the red moon appeared and poured a glow of blood over the water and the whole world.

But her scream had gone high and piercingly through the darkness, had travelled over the land and had reached the ear of the fisherman, who was watching his pole calmly and intently. The man started up, collected his thoughts, and it occurred to him that those two from just now had blundered into the water. Without reflecting further, he grabbed his mooring pole, which had a sharp hook on top, jumped out of the rowing boat onto the dyke and hurried along in the direction from which he thought he had heard the sound coming. The man, who heard no one and saw no sign, thought that he had already walked too far. He did not know what to do. Where had it happened? So he went on, a long way past the willow trunk. There was no sign of those two and cursing his helplessness, he went back in displeasure. Yet he stuck his pole in the water here and there because he was certain that they had drowned. But lo and behold, when he got back to the willow trunk, he saw a hat lying there. So, it had been here. And he immediately went down the dyke, ventured into the water above his ankles and searched with his pole in the depths.

As luck would have it within two minutes or so he pulled up a man. He dragged him coughing and gasping out of the water onto the dyke. Hendrik lay there like a bundle of rags and the water ran out of his mouth. The fisherman took him in his powerful arms and set him down with his back against the willow trunk. And then, with a 'now the other one', he began looking again. But he found nothing. The man felt in a proper quandary. What was he to do now? He looked round at Hendrik. His head hung pale on his black shoulders, it gleamed with wetness in the moonlight. It was frightening to see. Suddenly he fell forward. The fisherman leapt into action and without thinking of 'the other one', who had certainly been washed away, began slapping Hendrik's back and moving his arms. He tore open the coat and shirt and rubbed his wet, thin, cold chest with his heavy hand. And see! he moved an arm and raised his pale head in the moonlight.

Then the fisherman suddenly lifted him up, hung him on his broad back and walked with him into town. Hendrik's body, which was hanging limply and was still dripping with water, bumped and swung to and fro.

Scarcely had he reached the streets when a mass of people swarmed round the fisherman as he walked along. It was as if people rose out of the ground, and they walked along with him, pushing and shoving to see the dead man, whom they had just now allowed to pass by with an indifferent eye. They were children, men, women, and they clustered together, groaned, cursed, squeezed past each other, always hurrying to see the person over whom death had passed.

And when, recovered (thanks to the good offices of the physicians), pale, he lay sleeping with weak breaths under the white sheets, in the silent, white, poor little room, lit by a two-cent candle, his sisters came and made a terrible fuss.

They wept with happiness that their dear brother had escaped this cruel and unfair accident, and they would now have him with them again and the anguish and sorrow would be gone, now that she, 'that other one', was dead. For inwardly these two women were delighted that 'that other one' had not been rescued, and they considered it a punishment of God because she had wanted to tear their dear brother away from them.

And in the dancing candlelight they prayed that he might recover . . .

When morning was sifted out of the night, he moved. He opened his eyes and let his large black eyeballs roll in their sockets.

Then he remained lying still, looking straight at the white ceiling. In his half-sleep he felt the warmth of the bed around his flesh, which was cold inside and shivered. Was this the peace and happiness of death? . . . Yes, that was the coming happiness, because soon it would become still warmer, all through his body, and then he would come and melt into happiness. He found it pleasant waiting for that great moment. Imagining himself dead, not thinking of Begga, so dear to him, but waiting for the pleasure and delights of death, he was happy and wanted it to continue like that.

'How are you feeling?' asked the eldest sister, pleased.

He started out of his pleasurable feeling, looked at

her in surprise and stammered in astonishment: 'What are you doing here? . . .' And then suddenly he recognised his room, with the whitewashed walls. In a trice he saw the black crucifix above the bed, the portrait of his mother over the door and the two dirty black-framed engravings. Yes, yes, it was his room and his sisters were sitting praying with rosaries in their hands . . .

A raw cry broke loose from his throat. He was still alive! Hastily he felt himself, looked questioningly at his frightened sisters and then burst into loud weeping, sitting up in his bed. It was the disillusionment.

He wondered how he had got here and whether yesterday's death were not a dream . . . Yes, it had been a dream, from which he had unfortunately awakened. And again he felt life, from which just now he was so distant, crushing his heart like a marble block. And he wept because he was not yet dead. So it would be this evening that they had to do it. But then his saw his frightened sisters praying again. After all, then, something of unusual interest had happened to him? . . .

Just then his sister said: 'Oh poor thing, he can scarcely believe he's still alive.' Then he woke up for good. The words poured like flames in his ears. He quickly shot upright, crying fearfully: 'But what happened to me, you're sitting there looking at me as if it wasn't me? . . . What do you want? . . . Why are you praying? . . .'

And then they began telling him everything as they had heard it from the fisherman.

'Is it true . . . is it true, is it true after all?' He needed space, threw off the covers, jumped out of bed and fell weeping with his head on the table. So it hadn't been a dream. He could not think. His thoughts were like ash: when he tried to grasp them, they disintegrated.

'And she?' he asked suddenly.

And his sisters did not dare answer, for fear that he would feel they were glad about her death.

'And she?' he asked again in despair.

'Cannot be found,' said one.

And his body began shivering and shaking like a leaf, so that the light table on which his arms were resting creaked from the jolting . . .

'Come on, lad, back to bed, come on.' He did it. They gave him some light tea to drink.

So, she was dead, his Begga, whom he had loved so much, for whom he had suffered so much, she lay in unconscious death, released from worldly heaviness and misery, and he was left behind alone in the wide world, where there was no path for him, where he felt redundant, where he thought of himself as a curse, a false chord. And he tried to weep with grief, that he was not with her. He felt that he was trying to weep and knew he was lying to himself, for something had left him, he had left something of himself behind in that water. Could it be the invisible bond between their two hearts, that unknown force that drew them together, above everything? . . . Yes, that was it. He felt something had broken between him and her. Was it because she was dead? . . . Had death bitten through it? . . . He did not know what. But as fine and sharp as a pin he felt that he was glad he was still alive. And again, he began to prettify his cowardly attitude: now she was dead and according to him no longer felt anything, she was happy, and wasn't it because she felt happy that he was also? And now it seemed to him that all his former sorrow issued from her sorrow. And now he found it stupid that he had wanted to drown himself in order to be happy, to be happy, which he now found so easy and simple.

And there was a beneficent goodness in him. And she lay there alone in that water, she was dead and he felt happy. He remembered the promise of love and faithfulness, what they had sometimes wanted and worked at like a single being and then he saw the infinite rift that now opened between them.

Suddenly he felt his cowardice like a piece of ice and he burst into tears. He wept because she was dead, he wept because he no longer loved her.

The unknown bond between them had evaporated like a cloud.

But he resolved (the love that turned to pity) to pray for her, to pray a great deal and not to love another woman. Finally, he himself was pleased with this solution and without realising it dozed off to sleep . . .

The doctor woke him up when twilight was falling in the house. Immediately he was seized by great fear and his heart contracted. He was frightened of the approaching darkness. He never was usually. Was this because of his weakness? He hoped so. Why was he afraid? . . . He didn't know, but the white of the walls with the twilight on them was so awful, as he had never seen it before . . . The crucifix hung there so stupidly, and the engravings were like strange things.

From the window, through which he saw his garden and the mass of many town roofs, the grey sky, in which a wide yellow cleft gaped, was visible. He saw the cleft quickly close and then darkness immediately descended on the world. The angular figures of his sisters melted in the twilight. He again suddenly thought of her and imagined very well how she lay there in the cold water, pale and dead. He shivered and suddenly thought of her words, those terrible words: 'I think that if I had to lie alone in this water, I would rise up out of it to come and get you.' Sweat appeared on his forehead.

He shuddered and became afraid when he imagined that this might one day happen. His sister lit a candle, the scanty light scarcely reached the austere white walls and danced. Everything danced along with it. He let out a sigh of relief, for the darkness weighed on his heart like a piece of iron. He was glad there was light. No, she would not be able to put her dreadful words into effect, she was dead, and dead people can't do anything anymore.

His sisters cared for him and sat by his bed knitting white stockings. They did not say much and there was a great silence, in which the tick-tock of the hanging clock progressed slowly and snappily and the steel needles ticked between the callused fingers.

He had hoped that with the light his fear would disappear, but it welled up again, forcing and burrowing like a token of ill luck. He was in terror of the night and asked: 'You're not going to leave me alone tonight, are you?' They were surprised at his question . . . why would they not stay with him? But he omitted to say that he was afraid only in this house, in which he had lived for a year cut off from everyone and had never felt a shiver.

He would have liked to sleep in order not to know that it was evening. He said that he felt tired. His sisters cooked three poppyseed rolls on the stove and he soon fell asleep and in heavy dreams saw Begga's head white and big in the water and her eyes, in which a green light shone, kept opening and closing.

The next day, after a languid sleep, he got up. He

blamed the terror of the night before on the fever. He now felt rested, his senses sharp and his heart free.

His sisters, who had already prepared coffee on the stove, said to him that he must now leave this house and move back in with them. But he would have none of it. He had been so to speak chased out of their house and had sworn never to set foot in it again. He still hated them, though he omitted to say this and was able to make them understand very amicably that he was quite content and happy here on his own and was keen to continue living here like this. He would take up his lace pattern-making again and come and join them in the evenings and on Sundays.

His sisters went away reassured. After he had drunk the coffee, he went for a walk in the town park. The trees were bare and the leaves lay loose on the ground. The sky was fine blue. He sat down on a white bench, right in front of the smooth pond, and observed the noble pair of white swans. But why did he think so eternally of her? . . . And why did he always see this white head, with the green eyes in it?

It soon grew dark and then his heart began to shrink again and like a restless bumblebee round his head he constantly heard her threatening words.

He was sorry he was not at home now, now he would come into a dark house. He would have preferred to see the twilight thicken with his eyes; then before it was dark he would be familiar with the darkness and the evening would not be so oppressive. But why need he be afraid in his own house? . . . Oh, he didn't know, he felt, since he had been in the water, completely changed, as if he were no longer himself. He still believed there was something around him but didn't know what. He felt regret for not having agreed to living with his sisters. But he was too proud to bend his knee, though if they asked again he would agree. True, he hated them, but then he would not be so alone. He went into their house. They were still knitting the white stockings by the light of the porcelain lamp. He complained of pains in his loins, so that they would ask him to stay and sleep under their roof. But the eldest said with concern: 'Go home quickly, lad, and go straight to bed.'

He looked crestfallen and without saying more than 'good evening' he left. He could have wept with regret at having refused their offer. The streets were empty, with here and there still a brashly lit shop. He stopped and looked at those shops but did not see what was on display.

If only he were at home now! He would stroll around until he felt sleepy. He could not imagine how in the days before he was so indifferent to darkness. His heart felt constrained, as if a great misfortune were hanging over his head. He had the strange premonition that at home, in the dark room, something was awaiting him . . . He went further and thought of her pale face with green eyes. The lights went out irregularly and the last steps rang out in the cold street. And finally, he stood alone in the sleeping town with the night draped over it. He was still not sleepy but was shivering with cold. He saw the sky full of stars and behind the ponderous black tower flowered the light of the risen moon. It was very still and the wind had got up. He would walk a little more. But suddenly he turned around, gathered all his courage together and did not want to be afraid. Why must he be afraid? . . .

He arrived at his house, hastily opened and closed

the door, quickly lit the candle in the brass candleholder that always stood in the niche in the hall. And then he hurried to his room. The candlelight suddenly struck the white walls and made big shadows towards the extremities. He felt a shiver and started trembling. He tried to stop this trembling and go round the room, but his legs weighed like lead and were as powerless as in a nightmare. He would wait until it was over and would then quickly crawl into bed with the covers over his head. Meanwhile he saw the white walls and the long shadows and the candlelight that was as still as glass. He suddenly found that white so lugubrious that he immediately resolved to have the walls papered in bright red the following day. The trembling lessened and he moved the candle to make the shadow shorter. He was glad that this unknown thing of which he was so afraid did not appear.

It was just imagination. He undressed and was about to go to bed when suddenly the door creaked in the silence. He stood as if rooted to the spot and turned his head towards the sound. It was quiet again. Sweat beaded on his forehead. A new shudder suddenly seized him and it was as though his heart were being crushed in two iron fists. His teeth chattered and his legs wobbled. And he began trembling more quickly, mixed with strong convulsions. He was about to jump into bed, but suddenly he felt something pleasant inside his body, which stroked him sweetly and gave him salutary enjoyment.

He immediately devoted a curious attention to it, how it grew greater in him and sweeter and sweeter like vintage wines. He felt it moving in him like a soft silky veil, it itched and tickled like a feather on the soles of his feet. And it spread, very far, and it seemed to him that he was not big enough to contain this thing. It became like a porridge that swelled and became stiffer, and immediately the pleasure disappeared. It became wooden and fastened itself like millions of suckers and spread so that it seemed as if his intestines were made of iron. He felt his limbs stiffening, as if they were turning to stone. And it was alive, that unknown thing, it was alive and jolted through arms and legs and head. It hurt him. And suddenly it was as if there were another person in himself who was taking over his nerves, blood and feeling.

He did not know how it came about, but it seemed to be Begga. It seemed strange to him that his own head was hers, that in his arms he felt hers, and in his whole body her body. It was her heart beating inside him. Yes, yes, he felt very well that it was her! And with this awareness he was overcome with such terror that he began shouting and wanted to run away, but his arms, animated by that strange power, began hitting out, his head began to shake and his body to tremble.

And this thing pulled him from his place to the door, through the hall. He tried to resist, to grab hold of something, but it pulled him further and further. Suddenly terror cut through his heart like a knife, so that he leapt up with a powerful motion. But it would not let go of him. He began jumping, dancing and weeping, walked in despair and terror to and fro down the hall, opened the front door and went outside into the cold dark street. He walked on weeping, but it walked with him and he bumped against a wall and lay there unconscious. Windows opened, white upper bodies leaned out for a moment and soon there were people standing round him with sleep-contorted faces and dishevelled clothes. They carried him back to his bed. He lay there flat on his back, and people thought he was dead.

The doctor came and was able to say that it was a very serious attack of nerves. He gave him an injection and four people kept watch.

When he woke up later in the day and there was no one seated around his bed any longer, he immediately considered his position and felt his terror again. But when he saw the white walls marked with square patches of sun, it pulsed through his mind like clear water.

He smiled. Yes, he had been frightened, but he knew that this was only because of the dark. And then he felt frightened of the coming night.

But now that it was still day, he deluded himself that this evening he would be strong. He would wait for evening in the room, watch it become dark. That was how he thought it best to counter his fear. He ate a few mouthfuls of bread and thought of the strange occurrence of yesterday evening. It had been pure imagination. After all, Begga was in the water and the dead could not do anything. But he still regretted having heard her say those terrible words. She would have done better to stay silent, then he would not have felt that terror.

He stayed sitting at the table, thinking of Begga. It pained him to think of her and he tried to direct his thoughts to something else, but they stuck like barbs in her image. And he kept seeing this white, dead head, which he had once loved and which now horrified him . . .

He looked around to see if it were growing dark yet. The sunshine was already behind the trees and had withdrawn its light from the room. He again took up a position to await the evening, fight it and overcome it. But he knew it would take a while yet. He would read a book. But he was not able; he kept looking up to see if it was darker yet. He measured the approaching evening by seeing an engraving fading away in the twilight. Just a moment ago he had seen all its lines, which now had become shadowy and had melted into a mass. He thought that it was growing dark fast today. And he wished that all that had occurred had happened in the summer. Then it stayed light for a long time and everything was not as frightening. Autumn had already begun and the days just opened and closed, grey and black. The engraving now lost its shape and he immediately saw how it was already darker in the corners and how the deep spaces under the chest and the bed were completely black. He could almost no longer see the print of his book. Something squeezed his heart tighter. Why did he keep thinking of Begga the whole time? And now it was growing dark he began to doubt whether it was really her who made him feel herself within him. The engraving was hidden in the darkness and the trees in the garden were no longer visible. He was not yet afraid and smiled with self-satisfaction at the thought. But why could he not sit in candlelight just as well as in the dark? . . . He fetched the candle from the hall and lit it. He felt great relief; so, had he been afraid after all? . . . The room was lit again and he saw things familiar and clear as during the day.

But he blew the candle out again, for the only one he had in the house would soon be used up and then he would have to sit so long in the dark again, because it wasn't yet late.

It was pitch black. There hung a silence of Death and

he listened to hear if there were any noises. Yes, there went the dry tick-tock of the hanging clock like a heavy man's step. He listened but could not see its taut face. This sound that remained so dreadful and could not be silent became like an obsession. He stopped the pendulum. He thought he was calmer now, but now there was such a great, mysterious silence that he no longer dared breathe. What if that thing of yesterday evening came back again now?

He felt himself suddenly becoming so frightened that he lit the candle again. The flame danced crazily around the wick and plunged with arbitrary twists. The shadows plunged with them. That made it seem as if everything were alive. He now became really afraid.

The darkness had made him slowly afraid and he found that even worse. He did not dare to stay sitting down and stood up. And see, his legs started knocking again and his head danced on his body, and again he was full of that sweetness, like warm honey. He felt it growing, wanted to walk away, but it intoxicated him like strong wines and he could not leave. But he knew that after this sweetness the most terrible thing of all would come. And then he let out a raw cry, gathered all his strength and went into the street. He entered the first house he came across. It was the home of poor people, and all six of them were just sitting at table eating their evening meal. Hendrik fell to the ground, convulsing and as if rolled from here to there by an invisible hand. He cried and shrieked that Begga was alive in him. Now that the astonished people saw him like this a second time, they were convinced that he was enchanted. The man and his son, who were strong fellows, held the unfortunate man while the wife wiped the blood off his face, for his head had hit the stones so hard that there was a bloody gash above his left eye. And again, he gradually fell asleep, a deep heavy sleep. The fellow carried him home and stayed watching at his bedside in the dark.

At noon – it was raining and he wore a white cloth around his head to cover the wound – he went to the monastery of the white friars to have himself exorcised. The fellow who had looked after him last night had advised him to do so as soon as he awoke.

He believed now too that the unknown thing in him was the devil. And the white friars were the only ones who could save him from it. The monastery lay hidden in the solitude of the long silent streets. The brother porter led him into a small, high, white room, where all that was hanging was a large black cross. It was very quiet, as if it did not belong to the world. A friar came, a tall thin figure, consumed by prayer and penance. He listened with closed eyes and pursed lips to the young man's experiences.

The friar shook his head when Hendrik thought that it was Begga entering into him but confirmed his words when he talked of the devil. The friar told him to come back after sunset, when the power of evil rises. Hendrik went to his room, filled with joyful hope. He wished that it would soon be evening. He was convinced that only the friar could cure him. And when he imagined that it would not be over, that this unknown thing would stay with him forever . . . then . . . oh then! He felt hot and sweat broke out. Oh, then . . . then the first thing he would do would be to move house. He would not want to live with his sisters, since ultimately they were to blame for these wretched days of his. He hated them even more now. No, he would go to the big town and there stay out late in the brash cafés, drink lots of beer and wine until he was drunk and chat and drink with women until the morning came and when daylight dawned make for his bed. That was all that was left to rid himself of this unknown thing. But unfortunately he saw his plan shatter, as he had no money and without it he couldn't lead a drinking life. Then he decided to start working in the bakeries at night, where the ovens flared up, but oh, his health wasn't worth sixpence and he would soon be chased off.

But why was he thinking so far ahead? Wouldn't the friar cure him with powerful prayers and spells?

And very slowly evening came. He went to the monastery. It was still raining, a sad rustling rain. In the gleaming streets that were full of puddles a subtle, horrid cold hung about that bit through the clothes. He pulled his collar over his ears and went quickly. Well, it wasn't far and he did not think it worthwhile to take an umbrella with him.

Again he had to wait in the white cell, now that it was dark. He was frightened to stay in it and stood in the empty corridor in front of the door. The friar was not long, and he followed him into the chapel. The scent of incense caressed his face. In the darkness a sanctuary lamp was burning which rubbed its red light on the dull copper cupola of the Byzantine altar and on the two rows of white friars who, in the stalls facing each other, were cloaked motionless in their ample habits.

This startled him and he would have preferred to leave again.

The friar made Hendrik kneel before the altar where

he had to call sincerely upon the Lord and positioned himself behind him. The friar prayed in a coarse voice long Latin sentences and the other friars, without moving a crease of their habits, echoed him. Their words came as if from deep under the ground. Hendrik could not pray, he felt strangely troubled and listened to how their words buzzed like old bumblebees. What were they going to do with him shortly to drive the devil out of his body? . . . Would it be done with just those few words? . . . His blood froze with fearful curiosity. Suddenly it became still, so cruelly still, as if there were no one around him anymore. Had the friars left him alone in this dark, cold church? . . . He looked around in fear. They were still sitting motionless in the scanty red light like blocks of marble. Behind him stood the friar with his arms outspread. What were they going to do to him? . . . He heard steps. And three friars emerged from a small dark doorway. One carried a large burning candle and a censer, the second a thick book and the third a copper bucket with a brush. Now the candlelight illuminated those friars sitting motionless more brightly and made black shadows in the folds and a dark hollow under the hood, as if there were no head underneath. Hendrik had to stand up. With a short rustle of much heavy clothing the friars had also stood up. The friar who had led him in opened the book, which was resting on the chest of the friar carrying it. The candle lit the Gothic lettering of the pages.

And then the exorcism began. The friar put his left hand on the head of Hendrik, who was standing with his back to him, and with his right he made great signs of the cross at each sentence. He sang aloud, his eyes still fixed on the book. He sang the Latin words with a deep, dark voice, he held the sounds and made them resound so that they filled the whole chapel and their reverberation wandered through the dark. He did this with them all, as if he wanted to plant them forever in the stone walls. When he had sung three pages in this way, he suddenly fell into deep silence, took the brush, dipped it in the copper holy water container and then sprinkled the cold liquid over Hendrik's head and back, crying loudly like thunder an incomprehensible imprecation.

Hendrik went pale at the loud, heavy noise, but did not feel anything extraordinary moving in him. He thought it a useless game they were playing with him, since he knew that the unknown thing in him was too great and too powerful to be expelled by those hollow words and gestures. The candle was extinguished. He now had to lie flat on the ground, arms spread out like a crucified Jesus. All the friars gathered round him on their knees like round a dead person and began singing a long-drawn-out, high-pitched song that seemed to overarch him with stone bands. It sounded harsh and unnatural in the dark and there seemed to be no end to it . . . When he was tired from lying down and the cold of the stones had crept through his body and caused him great pain, they were silent. The friar who had exorcised him told him to go now, that it was over and that the devil had lost his power. He walked behind the friar, the others followed. In this way he was conducted through the corridors and let out. And then suddenly he was standing in the night again, alone with a heart shrinking with fear and hopelessness, and it was raining, still raining. He smiled bitterly, that thing was still alive in him and he felt that it was stronger than human might. But it was his punishment: he had not cooperated with grace . . . He went on through the rain and heard it rustling on the roofs and stones in the evening silence.

But he would not go home, because there the unknown thing would grow again and start to live. God! he was doomed to bear it forever! He would walk all night, through the rain and cold. He did not dare go and fetch his umbrella. He went along a few streets and felt happy to be out. The open air made the thing inside him be silent. He would now walk every night and sleep by day. It was already late; the streets were empty and the houses closed up. And now he heard how the sad rain descended on the whole town. It was like a great voice in the night. He went down many streets at a normal pace. When he crossed the bridges he heard the rain, which became more intense, spattering on the water. He liked this and sometimes stopped to listen. He became wet and saw his clothes gleaming when he passed a strange, dirty paraffin lantern.

It was dark, pitch black, it did not seem possible that the sun would ever again blaze from this blackness. The night was as if petrified over the world. Now and then a lonely clock sounded. It was the only sign that anything was still alive. He did not meet a single person. He was already far from home and reached the church. The building hid itself in the darkness of the night. But he heard the rain moving on the roof and the gargoyles pouring down the splashing water. He felt the wetness of his clothes on his back and he immediately had repeated shivers. The wet legs of his trousers stuck to him and the ends clumped and splashed on his shoes which were sucking up water. His socks were drenched and sodden and he could no longer feel his toes with the cold. Again, he saw Begga's large white head with the green eyes that opened and closed. He became very sad. Was it the sad sound of the rain that made the melancholy rise in his heart? . . . Oh, what was his life without Begga? . . . Why had he been glad that he had not died? How gladly he would have lain by her in the water! . . . Oh, now his whole life would be a persecution by that unknown, dark power, he would be lost in terror and despair and never know a peaceful hour again. Oh, why was he alive? And he felt a burning regret that had he awakened from the arms of death. He had rather be dead again. Large drops kept leaking from the brim of his hat, the cloth around his head had got wet and the wound was burning; he felt a heavy pain in his head.

He took the cloth off, but it stuck a little in the wound, which had opened again and began quietly to bleed. The blood leaked slowly down over his eye, over his cheeks, reached his chin and dripped onto his coat.

He held his hand on the wound. And he went on through the streets, and it rained, rained as if it would never stop. He had already been past the park three times, but he went on his way again, took other streets and finally came without knowing it to the fortifications, which with a double line of mature elms surrounded the silent town. Yonder before him, past rubbish and piles of stone, the open countryside spread wide and dark. He had also taken this route when he went to drown himself. He wanted to go as far as the bridge. At the end of the rubbish heaps he came to the Nete dyke. His shoes sucked up the water of the puddles and it soaked through and into his socks. And when he went onto the bridge, in the middle of the open fields, and stood there lonely and isolated in the wide, dark plain, he heard the sad rustling of the rain over the fields like a sustained sigh that rose from the earth. Involuntarily he walked on. And he began to weep at all his misery. He thought of all the vicissitudes of the past, of how everything in life was set against him. He felt like God's stepchild. Oh, it could all have gone so differently. Why couldn't he have been allowed to marry Begga? They could have been so happy. Suddenly a desire arose in him to be able to press a warm woman's body against his cold wet body. If he had married Begga, he would now be lying with her in a soft bed and be warm. He shivered with cold. The rain had completely drenched his clothes, the wet leaked over his bare back, he felt it running over his thin shivering thighs, down his legs, to join the other water in his shoes. The edges of his sleeves lay cold and heavy in his icy hands. His hat was as limp as a dishcloth and constantly leaked thick drops onto his shoulders, so that he felt it down to his bare skin. His shivering body was covered in gooseflesh. Oh, he was so cold, he was cold in his very soul. And the land, the distant dark land sighed and groaned.

The wet clothes rubbed rough and cold against his thin body. He would have been less cold naked than with all those heavily drenched clothes. He reached the willow trunk. He could scarcely see it in the darkness. He felt it, it was wet and slippery under his hand.

Why was that willow standing there? . . . And why had he himself come here? Now that Hendrik was standing where they had gone to drown themselves a shudder he could not fathom went through him. Was it because here death had lived in him? . . . Or was it because Begga had said that she would rise up out of this water to get him? . . . At this last thought he felt a strong shock in his chest. His legs wobbled. He wanted to go, as he felt that it was beginning again, but a shiver flashed through his body and he felt rooted to the spot. And again, that seductive sweetness came up and something inside pulled him towards the water. He saw the danger of it. And with a powerful gesture he threw his arms round the willow trunk and began crying and shouting. It sounded dreadful in the hollow black night and joined in with the sad rustling of the rain. Hendrik wept, stamped to keep the invisible thing away from him and cried for help, appealed to God, his mother and all the saints, but the power inside him expanded mercilessly and planted its strength in all the tissues of his body.

He pressed his arms firmer round the slippery rough trunk, and sobbed, wept and howled. But the unknown thing crept into his arms and went slowly but surely to his hands, always pulling towards the water's edge. Hendrik pressed his nails in the flesh of his hands, so that he bled, but the invisible force calmly lifted the fingers apart, prised the hands apart and dragged him with a strong jolt backwards into the water. The water opened up and closed, without many waves. And a moment later there was nothing more to be heard than the rain, the eternally rustling rain. It was like a great sigh rising from the bowels of the earth into the dark night.

*These stories were written in Lier, 1909.*